WHEN ART Rises
LIVING IN CIN

LORRAIN ALLEN

Copyright © 2020 by Lorrain Allen

Published by Lorrain Allen

All rights reserved

ISBN: 978-1-7342309-2-5

No part of this book may be reproduced in any form or by any electronic or mechanical means, including information storage and retrieval systems, without written permission from the author, except for use of brief quotations in a book review.

This book is licensed for your personal enjoyment only. This book may not be resold or given away to other people. If you would like to share this book with another person, please purchase an additional copy for each reader. Thank you for respecting the work of this author.

This book is a work of fiction. All names, characters, places, and incidents either are a product of the author's imagination or are used fictitiously. Any resemblance to events, locales, or persons, living or dead, is coincidental.

The author acknowledges all song titles, song lyrics, film titles, film characters, trademarked statuses, and brands mentioned in this book are the property of, and belong to, their respective owners. The publication/use of these trademarks are not authorized/associated with, or sponsored by the trademark owners.

Lorrain Allen is in no way affiliated with any of the brands, songs, musicians or artists mentioned in this book.

Edited by: Maggie Kern
https://www.facebook.com/Ms.Kedits

Proofread by: Emily Hainsworth
http://www.emilyhainsworth.com

Proofread by: Novel Nurse Editing
https://NovelNurseEditing.com/

Formatted by: Brenda Wright
https://www.facebook.com/FormattingDoneWright/

author's note

This book features an out-of-control, jealous antihero, abuse, graphic language, explicit sex scenes, and other subject matters some readers might find triggering. Arthur King is not a comfortable antihero to read about. If you expect a redeemable antihero this book is not for you. He does NOT grovel or beg. While the setting of the book is in a high school environment, its recommended reading age is eighteen+. Scan QR code to view content warning.

playlist

"Kiss it Better" – Rihanna
"I Knew You Were Trouble" – Taylor Swift
"Wrecking Ball" – Miley Cyrus
"Love Me Like You Do" – Ellie Goulding
"Crazy In Love (Fifty Shades of Grey Remix)" – Beyoncé
"Haunted" – Beyoncé
"Dangerously in Love" – Destiny's Child
"Power Trip" – J. Cole featuring Miguel
"Sure Thing" – Miguel
"Bed" – J. Holiday
"All The Time" – Jeremih featuring Lil Wayne and Natasha Mosley
"Dive In" – Trey Songz

PROLOGUE

ART

As I peer down at my three-year-old brother lying in the superhero-painted casket, guilt consumes me like a festering wound, slowly poisoning my body. I don't cry. I don't know how to. He looks as if he's sleeping, like at any moment he'll open his bright clear-green eyes and ask me to play with him. His black eyelashes lie against his pale skin. I can barely glance in the mirror anymore without seeing Cole staring back at me. We have the same black hair, eye color, and facial features—courtesy of our father. He was so full of life and curiosity, but now he's an empty shell. It takes everything in me not to grip his shoulders, to shake him, to demand he wake up. All of his favorite action figures and other toys lie in the casket with him. Large photographs of him smiling, playing, and doing various activities surround the casket. I would give anything to have the ability to manipulate time.

This isn't real. It can't be real. It's a nightmare. Wake up—please wake up.

I will it to be true. I squeeze my eyes shut, then slowly open them again, confirming my worst fears: this is reality.

Fuck reality.

The day I found Cole floating in the water, my life was shattered. I searched the huge mansion for thirty minutes before deciding to head to the backyard. I didn't think he would be there, since he knows not to go near the pool alone. He was just learning to swim and needed a lot more practice before swimming without any assistance. I immediately dived into the water to retrieve Cole. His small body was ice cold. I screamed for one of my friends to dial nine-one-one. I worked on trying to revive him until paramedics arrived. Later, I would find out that nothing I did would've saved him. Cole had been in the pool for eighteen hours. He was pronounced dead at two o'clock. I might as well have been in the pool beside him, lifeless. I haven't been eating, sleeping, or showering. I know I resemble the walking dead. I may look calm on the outside, but that's merely a persona. If one more person says, "I'm sorry for your loss," they're going to get a broken nose. Inside I feel like a volcano ready to erupt, and everyone around me will be burned alive by the lava.

I failed him when he needed me the most. I was supposed to watch over him, protect him. If it wasn't for me, he'd still be alive, but I'm a selfish motherfucker—a fifteen-year-old drug addict, my narcotic of choice: *cocaine*. I spent the night before I found Cole fucking, drinking, snorting coke, and partying. It was a Saturday night, the nanny had a family emergency, my mother was out fucking only God-knows-who, and my father was at his office, attempting to hide from his fucked-up life, scheming wife, and controlling father. Giving them the label of mother and father is a stretch. More times than not, my mother acted as if my brother and I didn't exist. She doesn't have the maternal gene. I was raised by my nanny until I became old enough to look after myself. For the most part, I have zero adult supervision.

My father is a weak man, controlled by his father like a puppet and used as a doormat by his manipulating wife. He was completely infatuated with her, acting the besotted fool, I've been told. She was nineteen when they met and he was forty, thinking with his dick instead of his brain. He didn't stand a chance against her alluring hazel eyes and strawberry-blond locks. His sin was lust—hers, greed. A match made in a fucked-up paradise. A year later, they were married. The following year, I was born. My father had a severe stroke the night after learning of Cole's death. He's in a comatose state with little hope of recovery. My mother lavishes unwanted attention on me now—no doubt she's just as guilt ridden as me.

I was once a rising football star until I started skipping school and hanging out with a crowd much older than me.

God, please take me instead.

My plea goes unanswered. I can't live with this. It's tearing me apart. The church is filled to the brim with mourners here to say their final farewell to my little brother. When I arrived, I walked straight to his casket and haven't moved. Someone grasps my shoulder, but I don't turn to see who it is.

"Art, the service is about to start," Uncle Ricky says.

He pulls me to the first pew where I sit down.

Sometime later, I'm in the limousine with my uncle and his son, Josh, as well as my grandfather and mother, heading to the cemetery. No one says a word. The tension is thick. I can count on my hand the number of times I've seen my uncle and cousin over the years. Josh and I bumped heads the first time we met, and since that day we've had an unspoken rivalry between us. My uncle is lucky. He got away from this fucked-up family and never looked back. When my grandfather failed to control my uncle, he sank his talons into my father. The old man is a self-made millionaire who dominates the real estate industry, leading him to open five-star hotels along the East Coast called The Falcon with plans to expand globally. Now that my father had a stroke with little hope of recovery, he wants to bring Ricky back into the fold, but he's not interested. Neither am I. My grandfather can kiss my ass. The entire service was a haze. I don't recall any of it.

I walk to the gravesite, feeling like a death-row inmate.

As I walk through the valley of the shadow of death...

The reverend reads a few verses from the Bible. Once the service is concluded, family and friends walk to their vehicles. Most will be driving to my home for the repast. I never understood the point of a repast. I don't want to eat or sit around and talk with people. I want to be left the fuck alone.

"Art, are you ready to go?" Ricky squeezes my shoulder.

"I'm not leaving. Not until the casket is covered."

"Okay, I'll stay with you."

He walks over and talks to my mother before coming back to stand beside me. The sound of the dirt hitting the casket is going to haunt me for the rest of my life.

Ricky and I arrive at the mansion a little later.

"I'm going to my bedroom."

"I'll be up in a few minutes to check on you."

I feel sick to my stomach as I race up the staircase. Once I reach the privacy of my bedroom, I shut and lock the door before stripping out of my suit. I walk over to the dresser to retrieve my pocketknife from the top drawer, then sit on my bed. There is one universal fact that can't be ignored.

I don't deserve to be alive.

I slit one wrist and then the other. The knife falls to the floor from my numb fingers. I lie back on the soft mattress. There's a knock on my bedroom door.

"Art?" Ricky calls.

I feel drowsy, like I've been drugged.

The knock comes again. I'm slipping away into oblivion, where I want to be. After a few loud bangs, the door swings open.

When Art Rises: Living in Cin

"My God! Art, what have you done?"
Darkness envelopes me, and finally the pain is gone.

CHAPTER one

Three years later

ART

I watch snowflakes float down from the bright blue sky while sitting at my desk located in the back of the classroom.

"Art, would you like to read your essay?" Mr. Jared, the English Literature teacher, asks.

Fuck, I don't need this shit. It's the last day of school before winter vacation. When I rolled out of bed this morning, I didn't brush my hair or shower. I'm impressed with myself for actually taking the time to at least wash my face and brush my teeth. My uniform is wrinkled, the shirt open at the collar with my tie hanging loosely around my neck. It's the last class before lunch.

I'm getting through this damn day by the skin of my teeth.

Usually teachers don't bother me since my grandfather wrote a big fat check just to get me into this school. Bribery is something he excels at. I've been kicked out of four schools, including one military, since being released from rehab two years ago, so the old man must've been extremely generous. Blackwood Academy is one of the most expensive private schools in Boston, Massachusetts. The offspring of the rich and famous are enrolled here. I have the same financial status as them, but that's where the similarities end. My appearance alone should've made it impossible for me to be accepted.

I have small stainless-steel hoops hanging from my ears, as well as a frenulum, nose, lip, and tongue piercings. My tattoos include flames covering my right arm up to my neck, a skull on my right pectoral, a heart with a knife through it on my left, a semicolon behind my left ear, and the last one is an image of Cole covering my entire back with the sun shining behind him. Just before Thanksgiving break, the class was given an assignment to select an important figure in history who made a significant impact on how the United States operates today. It's about a week before Christmas, Cole's favorite holiday, so I sure as hell wasn't thinking about a fucking assignment. What I really want to do is buy cocaine. The urge is beating at me, wearing me down, and I want to give in.

I can't sleep at night because my little brother haunts my dreams. The conclusion of the nightmare is always the same.

"Help me! Please, help me, Art!"

"I'm coming, Cole. Hold on!" I yell.

The faster I run, the farther away the pool seems to be. In the distance, I can see Cole fighting to stay above the water. I pump my legs harder, pushing my body to the limit. Sweat drips down my face, but I'm not making progress. The fight in Cole lessens with each second that passes.

"Don't give up, Cole!" I shout frantically.

His body disappears under the surface. The silence is deafening.

I always wake up right after that moment in a cold sweat, my heart pounding in my chest. With the nightmare being my constant companion, it's no wonder I'm sleep deprived.

"No, I don't," I reply.

"Why not?"

"Because I didn't complete the assignment," I reply nonchalantly.

A few of my classmates snicker.

"Art, you're skating on thin ice. Do you want to graduate?"

"I really don't give a fuck if I graduate or not, Mr. Jared."

"That's not a good attitude to have."

"But it's the only one I've got."

Kade cuts in. "Mr. Jared, you shouldn't waste your breath on scum like him. He's a lost cause."

He's sitting a few seats over from me.

"Do you want to say that to my face?" I ask.

"Whoa, gentleman. Let's be civilized to one another," Mr. Jared cautions.

"Arthur, I smelled a little something when you walked by me, and I just wanted to know if you washed your ass this morning. From the state of your appearance, I'm assuming the answer is no." Owen chuckles.

That statement causes the entire class to erupt into laughter.

"That's the scent of your mother. I was in her pussy all night."

"You motherfucker," Owen growls.

"It's time for your ass whooping," Kenny announces.

If I get into one more fight this school year, I'll be expelled, but if Kade and these motherfuckers want to continue the beef, I'm game. They thought I would be an easy target to bully since I have no friends and keep to myself, but they are mistaken. Though it'll be three against one, I'm not scared. I'm looking forward to the confrontation. I'm instantly on alert, ready to throw down.

"Enough!" Mr. Jared bellows.

Kade, Owen, and Kenny are on the lacrosse team, so they're pretty buff. I may not play football anymore, but I'm just as big due to my nights spent working out to avoid sleeping.

"Mr. Jared, isn't it unsafe for someone with a history of mental illness to attend school with normal kids?" Kade asks in false concern.

"Everyone knows you wear those leather wristbands to cover up the scars from your suicide attempt. How about you finish the job so you can join your dead brother?" Kenny asks.

I snap. I don't give a fuck what anyone says about me, but my brother is off-limits. I stand, pick up the desk, and launch it across the room to strike Kenny in the face. He's out cold. Shocked gasps and loud cheers fill the classroom. I hear Mr. Jared call for security on the radio. Kade and Owen rush me. I sidestep them, hitting Owen in the throat. He drops to his knees, grabbing his neck. Two down, one more to go. This is light work. I duck down when Kade swings his fist at my face. I come up with a hard jab to his side, making sure I put all my strength behind the hit. The cracking sound, coupled with his cry of pain, is satisfying. I broke the fucker's ribs.

Two security officers enter the room.

"I should've known it was you." Tony sighs.

"Well, you know me, Tony. My day isn't complete unless I fuck shit up." We're on a first-name basis since we've become so well acquainted.

"Let's go. You know the drill."

I follow Tony out of the classroom without a fight while the other security officer and Mr. Jared attend to those bastards. Well, this will be my last day at Blackwood Academy.

CHAPTER two

ART

I sit in a chair outside of Principal Patrick's office. I'm sure he already called my mother. I'm positive she and the old man will be waiting for me when I arrive home. I scrub a hand down my face. I don't want to deal with this bullshit. I have zero fucking patience right now. I should get out of here. What's the point in waiting around when I already know what he's going to tell me? I stand, determined to leave, but Principal Patrick's door opens.

"Art, please come inside and have a seat."

I stroll into his office. "I'll stand."

"You do know this is the last straw, don't you?"

I shrug my shoulders. "So what else is new?"

"You can't go through life with this 'I don't care' attitude of yours."

Attempting suicide was the coward's way out. I deserve to live every fucking day with the death of Cole beating at my conscience relentlessly. Misery is my constant companion from sun up to sun down. I don't deserve peace.

"Well, that's exactly what I plan to do."

"I know the last couple of years have been tough with the passing of your brother—"

"I'm not listening to this." Any talk about Cole is dangerous territory. I'll go the fuck off.

"I'm sorry. I know that's a tough topic for you."

"Fuck you."

"This is a serious situation. Some of Kade's ribs are broken, Kenny has a concussion, and Owen can barely talk. They're being transported to the hospital by ambulance. You could be charged with assault."

"My grandfather has more money than God. Their parents' silence will be bought. Money makes the world go round. Anyway, I didn't start the fight. I just finished it. I have the right to defend myself."

"Witnesses say you struck first."

"Well, that's what happens to motherfuckers who mention my brother." I smirk.

"This isn't a joke."

"That's where you're wrong. Life is one big fucking joke with a shitty punch line."

"You're expelled, effective immediately."

"Tell me something I don't know."

"Tony will escort you to your locker to get your personal things."

"The only place I want to be escorted to is the front door."

I leave his office with Tony trailing behind me.

"Wait," Tony calls a second before I'm about to pass through the exit.

I continue walking forward, not breaking my stride. "What?"

"You're a good kid. You can be anything you want in life. Don't ruin it."

"I don't have a future," I reply.

I walk across the school grounds and hop on my motorcycle, a BMW R1200GS. I rev the engine and zoom out of the parking lot. I never wear a helmet because I'm not afraid to die. I'm afraid to live. I don't plan to go home to face my mother and the old man just yet. They'll have to wait a few hours to feed me their bullshit speeches.

The sun has been set for hours by the time I arrive home. I enter the code at the gates before continuing towards the big structure. When I enter the garage, I see my grandfather's Bugatti Chiron next to my mother's Ferrari LaFerrari Aperta. I kill the engine, then walk through the mudroom to enter the kitchen where the two of them are sitting at the island bar, waiting for me.

Figures.

My mother has a distressed look on her face, but the old man's face is the complete opposite. He's furious.

"Arthur, shall we have a conversation about what occurred in class today?" He refuses to call me by my nickname.

"No, I'd prefer if we didn't have this conversation at all."

By the time I was released from rehab, my mother had moved. There's no way I would've been able to live in the same place where Cole died. Though the residence is spacious, it's nowhere near the size of the mansion where we used to live. There's a pool, but I don't go near it. I haven't been in a pool since that day. My therapist tried to help me overcome that fear to no avail. Going to a therapist was a waste of time and money. I'm still the same fucked-up person.

My grandfather has power of attorney over my father since his stroke. He's been a resident of a nursing home since the day he was discharged from the hospital. The doctors said he'll never make a full recovery. It's a good thing my grandfather has control over all my father's businesses and investments. My mother is a trophy wife who doesn't know the first thing about business. Her job is to sit and look pretty. I bet she's thrilled she doesn't have to pretend to be the doting wife anymore, free to fuck her way through the entire male population of Boston. She's a shitty wife and mother. She hasn't been to visit my father once, but then again, neither have I, so that makes me a shitty son. The old man pays all the monthly bills and deposits money into our separate checking accounts on a weekly basis.

I walk past the island bar, intending to leave the kitchen.

"Art, don't leave," my mother demands.

"Who's going to stop me?"

"You can't continue to function like this!" my grandfather shouts.

"What are you going to do after you graduate high school? You don't have the GPA to get accepted into college. You've been expelled from several schools. It's time for you to grow up!" my mother yells.

I turn to face her. "So now you want to pretend like you give a fuck about being a mother when I'm nearly eighteen? It's too late for that."

"Don't you dare talk to me like that." Her voice wavers.

Here come the damn waterworks.

"Don't you have a dick appointment? Your main squeeze must not be doing his job. Maybe you should get another one."

"That's enough!" my grandfather roars.

"I'm just getting started," I reply.

Tears begin to roll down her cheeks.

"She knows if she'd been home that night instead of spreading her legs, Cole would still be alive."

A loud sob leaves her mouth.

Good, the guilt can slowly kill us both.

The old man moves swiftly towards me with a raised hand, as if to strike.

"Watch it. You don't want to do that." My voice is calm, low... deadly.

"What happened to Cole was a tragic accident. It's no one's fault," my grandfather says.

That's where you're wrong.

"I've been in touch with your uncle," my mother says. "He's agreed to let you finish out your senior year in North Carolina with him."

The old man's head whips in her direction. "What?"

"I'm not going," I reply at the same time my grandfather says, "He's not going."

"You're out of control, and I can't handle you."

"You can't make me go."

"You can either move in with your uncle or your grandfather, but you can't stay here anymore. This is for your own good."

"Since one son is gone, why not get rid of the other one? You can finally have your freedom."

"I love you, Art. I want the best for you. This decision wasn't made lightly. You need a change of environment, somewhere peaceful. Your uncle's sweet potato farm will be perfect. You can reconnect with your cousin. He assures me it'll be the best place for you to overcome your demons."

"I like my demons. They're my constant companions."

"You can stay with me."

Fuck no.

"I'd rather take my chances in North Carolina," I say over my shoulder, leaving the kitchen.

He controlled my father like a puppet, but I refuse to let him pull that shit with me. I'll simply lie low until the end of the school year, unless somebody fucks with me. Then that's another story.

CHAPTER three

Cin

"Please tell me you're joking, Dad." Josh groans.

We're in the dining room, eating dinner. It's Christmas Eve.

One big happy family.

Things are about to get heated. The fights between Josh and his father are always epic. My mom's left eye twitches, which happens whenever she's on edge. She's attempting to get Ricky's attention from where she sits at the opposite end from him. She's a bundle of nerves during confrontations. I eat the *arroz de Braga* I cooked, not letting their argument bother me. I've never let the almost daily tug-of-war that happens between Ricky and Josh get to me.

After my mom and dad broke up, we relocated from Phoenix, Arizona, to Longhorn, North Carolina, so we could be closer to our family. It's awesome that I'm able to develop more of a relationship with Aunt Katrina and my cousins, Lilah and Dionte. Before the move, we barely saw each other. Lilah and I are both seventeen, so we have a lot in common. Dionte is a thirteen-year-old boy who has no interest in spending time with his older female cousin, but he's a good kid. Katrina's husband, Thomas, who's the local vet, introduced Mom to Ricky. They were inseparable from that day forward. My mom and aunt are down with the swirl. Ricky asked my mom to move in with him after only eight months of dating.

In the beginning, Josh and I hated each other. We didn't acknowledge each other at school and barely spoke a word at home unless we were arguing. We've actually come to physical blows a few times. He wanted Mom and me gone. Josh has mommy issues. His mom decided she didn't want to be a mom anymore, so one day she never came home, but she left a note. She literally disappeared off the face of the earth, and Ricky hired a private investigator to find her. Josh's and my dislike of each other caused a strain on Ricky and Mom's relationship.

Eventually, we came to an unspoken truce when I started dating his best friend, Trevor. The only downside to Trevor and me becoming an item is that it caused a rift between Lilah and me because she had a thing for him—a sentiment he did not return. In time, we were able to patch up our relationship. Lilah is a part of the "in" crowd, along with Josh. Instant popularity is definitely something I wasn't used to, but I like it very much. Classmates greet me as I walk through the halls and want to become my friend. Josh is one of the most popular boys in school, being the captain of the football and basketball team. To the girls at Central High School, he's prime real estate. He's tall with a lean muscular build, black hair, and dark-blue eyes.

Trevor plays football, too, but totally sucks ass at basketball. I was completely surprised that Trevor would want someone like me. Not that I'm butt ugly or anything, but I'm far from a beauty queen. He's not as tall as Josh at around five foot nine with a muscular frame, light amber-colored hair, and the most beautiful bright blue-green eyes I've ever seen. He's the essential boy next door. About a year ago, we broke up for two months because I didn't like the person he became when he got drunk. But he slowed down a lot, so we got back together. I'm a tomboy through and through. Hoodies, loose jeans, and Chuck Taylors are my clothing of choice during the cooler months. In the summer, T-shirts, shorts, and flip-flops are my best friends. The only girly thing about me is my black, long, wavy hair with pink highlights—my best asset—which stops right above my ass. I'm five foot two, one hundred and five pounds soaking wet. I have no ass or breasts to speak of. I have light cream-colored skin, courtesy of my Brazilian father.

"He's coming. The decision is final."

"You can't be serious!"

"I'm serious as a heart attack. He'll be here on Saturday," Ricky replies sternly.

"I live here too. I have a right to be included in decisions affecting me!" Josh shouts.

"Art has been going through a tough time since Cole's death. He's spiraling down a dark path, and I know I can help him. He needs to be surrounded by love."

Neither Ricky nor Josh talk much about their family. In Ricky's office, I saw a picture of him along with two other men. The similarities between the three are uncanny. I guessed they were his father and brother. Something terrible must've happened to cause a rift between them. Mom and Ricky had been dating for about a year when his nephew, Cole, tragically lost his life. He didn't want us to go to the funeral, so we stayed behind. I did overhear that Cole's older brother, Art, attempted suicide by slitting his wrists.

Josh laughs sarcastically. "Surrounded by love? This is fucking bullshit."

"Hey, watch your mouth!" Ricky yells.

"You let the devil in your house, you'll get burned."

"That's enough. He's coming to stay with us!" Ricky bangs his fist on the table.

Josh leans back against his chair, crossing his arms across his chest like a two-year-old.

"I'll need you to help me clear out the spare bedroom before Art gets here. The furniture is being delivered on Friday morning. I want to have everything done by Saturday so he'll feel welcomed."

Josh clenches his jaw.

"Cin, can you help too?" Mom asks.

"Sure."

"I'll cook a special dinner on Saturday night. I've been eyeing this new recipe I want to try," she announces enthusiastically.

Oh God, no, please help us all.

The conversation stops as we all zero in on my mom. She can't cook worth shit. That's why we're eating Christmas dinner over at Thomas and Katrina's tomorrow evening. Either Ricky or I do all the cooking. My grandmother on my father's side is a great cook and taught me very well when we lived in Phoenix. I spend every summer there, though I don't see my father as much as I'd like since he's a CDL driver. He's on the road most of the time. That's why my parents decided to call it quits. Also, Mom and my grandmother constantly bumped heads.

"Whatever you cook, I'm sure he'll love it," Ricky replies.

"I'm outta here." Josh leaves the table.

Ricky closes his eyes, rubbing his temples before letting out a long sigh. My mom leaves her chair to stand behind him and massage his tense shoulders. He places a soft kiss on her hand.

"Don't worry. It'll be okay. Cin and Josh didn't get along at first. Give it a month," Mom says.

"I hope you're right, and I hope I'm doing the right thing by bringing him here. Maybe I'm in over my head. Maybe he can't be helped."

"He can be helped. Like you said, he needs to be surrounded by love."

My mom kisses Ricky's lips when he lifts his head towards her. That's my cue to leave. I don't want to see this.

"I'm going for a run," I say, leaving the table.

"Okay, don't be gone too long," she tells me.

"Mom, you know I have to get ready for track season. It starts in about two months."

"Fine, just be careful. I don't like when you go running at night."

"I'll be fine," I say, kissing her cheek before leaving the dining room.

I climb the stairs, then turn left before stopping at Josh's door. I knock lightly.

"Go away!" he yells.

"It's me."

"Come in."

He's lying on his bed, tossing a football towards the ceiling, then catching it on the way back down.

"Will it be so bad to have your cousin living here?"

"You don't know him. He's a douchebag. On the rare occasion we visited our wacko family, he would always play some type of cruel joke on me. I remember one time he superglued my hands to my hair while I slept."

I chuckle a little.

"It's not funny, Cin. I had to get a really low buzz haircut after that. I was teased relentlessly."

"Come on, you were little kids."

"He and his sick friends tied me to a tree and left me there. Kids don't do shit like that. He's all kinds of twisted. I was happy when our visits stopped."

"Maybe he's changed. Just give him a chance."

"I don't want to give him a chance."

"You gave me one."

"That's different. My best friend fell for you."

This is one stubborn boy. "Well, like your father said, it's happening."

"Don't remind me."

"I'm going for a run. Goodnight."

I enter my bedroom. Ricky and Mom's master bedroom is on the right side of the staircase while the bathroom, linen closet, and Josh's and my bedrooms are on the left. On the ground level is Ricky's office, a spare room—now to be Art's bedroom—kitchen, living and dining room, and a full bathroom. There's a half bathroom in the basement along with the washer and dryer.

I've been in track and field since elementary school, but I didn't get really good until my sophomore year in high school. I won State that year and my junior year. I was widely recognized and given a scholarship to attend Lexington University in California. Trevor applied there and at a few other universities in the surrounding area so we can be near each other. I run the one-, two-, and four-hundred-meter races. I plan to win State again this year. I put on a hoodie over my T-shirt and change out of my sweatpants in favor of leggings. I slide my feet in a pair of sneakers before making my way downstairs and out the front door.

I look out at the three-hundred-acre land used for sweet potato farming as I complete a few stretches on the wraparound porch. I didn't know the first thing about sweet potato farms when I first relocated here, but I fell in love with the process and willingly help Ricky with the harvest every year. I'm going to assist Ricky and his employees in planting the slips again in April.

Harvest will begin in late August and end in November, but I'll be in college this time around. There are two other buildings stationed to the right of the house with the fields to the left. One is used to cure the sweet potatoes after harvest. The other is used to store the sweet potatoes after curing and the slips for winter. When Ricky receives orders from grocery stores, I help to rinse and pack them. My mom is a math whiz, so she's in charge of all the accounting stuff. I finish my stretches, then take off at a steady, brisk pace.

ART

"You're the first visitor Kyle has had since his arrival. May I ask who you are?"

"I'm Art, his son," I reply, following the nurse down the hall.

"My name is Octavia. I'm the head nurse in this ward. When I was told Kyle had a visitor, I had to come see for myself. Though your father has some cognitive abilities and can talk a little, he's rarely responsive, so I don't want you to get your hopes up."

Hope is a fucking fantasy to me. It doesn't exist. If it did, I'd already be dead.

I don't know what the fuck I'm doing here. I felt compelled to visit him before leaving for North

Carolina, like this would be the last opportunity to be able to.

"Okay, here we are."

I peek inside the open door to see a figure sitting in a chair, facing the window. The room is devoid of life and color. No paintings on the walls, no family photos, and no vase filled with flowers on the small table by the queen-sized bed. The old man has the means to put him in an upscale facility. It's obvious he chooses not to.

Part of me wants to race inside the room and wrap my arms around him in a tight hug, a lost little boy needing his father. The other part of me wants to rant and rave about what a pathetic bitch he is while beating the shit out of him. He should've put my mother and grandfather in their place a long time ago. He doesn't realize how much power he had over them.

"Go on in. He may not show it, but I know he'll be excited to see you on the inside."

I step through the door and remain there.

Fuck, I should just leave. No, man the fuck up and face him.

I grab the chair to the right of the door and slowly approach my father. I put it directly in front of him then sit down. His hair is almost snow white. Deep, defined wrinkles cover his face, neck, and hands. The morning I found Cole's lifeless body floating in the pool caused a chain reaction of misery and despair. I would give anything to turn back the hands of time. I replay the night in my mind over and over and over again. He was fighting for his life, petrified. I wonder what his last thought was. Did he think about me? Did he call out my name? When my brother took his last breath, I was getting high, fucking some nameless bitch.

Why, God? Why? I want to die too. I swear I can't live with this pain anymore. It's driving me insane.

My father doesn't acknowledge me, but I don't expect him to. He's staring slightly above my head, his mouth slack.

"Do you know who I am?"

Nothing.

"Look at me."

Still, he gives no reaction.

"August thirtieth," I say.

The day Cole died. His eyes slowly focus on me, and there's a spark of recognition in them. Tears glisten in his eyes before running down his cheeks.

"You were never around, but you should've been." I start crying like a pussy, but I can't control my emotions. "Damn you, damn her, and damn me. We failed him. It should be us in the ground."

He opens his lips, attempting to speak, but unintelligible sounds leave his mouth.

"What are you trying to say?"

"Sorry," he says in a cracked, barely audible voice.

I lean forward in the chair, clutching his face and looking into his eyes. "Being sorry isn't going to bring Cole back!" I yell.

We deal with the loss of Cole in our own ways. My mother chooses to pretend he never existed, my father hides inside his own mind, and I attempted suicide.

He cries harder.

I remove my hands from his face, leaning back against the chair. I wipe the tears from my cheeks.

"I don't know if I'll ever be back to see you again, Dad. I'm going to live with Ricky for a while but after that, who knows. Goodbye."

I leave the room without looking back.

I exit the facility and hop onto my motorcycle to beat a path to North Carolina. The cold air whips across my face as the miles fly by. Mommy Dearest already had my stuff delivered to my uncle's house. I didn't seek her out before leaving this morning. Her car was in the garage, which is surprising because it's rare for her to stay home on a Friday night. I guess she wanted to play the role of mother by seeing me off. The old man tried to persuade me to move in with him a few more times, afraid my uncle is going to turn me against him, but I refused.

I made it through another Christmas without *him*. I stayed in bed with the lights off. Grief never goes away or gets easier like some people claim. The urge to buy cocaine consumed my every thought until I finally left home on a mission to get high. Before I made it to my destination, I came to my senses. That's a dark path I don't care to venture down again. I parked my motorcycle on a side street then took off running. I ran until my body shut down and my mind became numb. I collapsed to the cold hard ground and crawled to the side of a building to lean against it. That's where I stayed for several hours before walking back to retrieve my motorcycle. There are three days that bring me to my lowest: August thirtieth, December twenty-fifth, and February fifth—Cole's birthday.

I remember the day he entered this world. My nanny brought me to the hospital. I was so excited to meet him. He was a wrinkled weird-looking little thing, but that didn't matter to me. I was a proud big brother. I was allowed to sit in a chair and hold him. I thought to myself, *I'll always protect him. I'll always be there for him. I'll be the best big brother.* But I wasn't. There are only two aspects of my life now—*before* Cole and *after* Cole. Before he died, my life was filled with limitless possibilities, but after he died, my life became an all-consuming darkness. Now every day I wake up hoping it's going to be my last day. If only I'd cut a little bit deeper, I would be six feet under right now.

CHAPTER five

ART

By the time I arrive at Ricky's house, it's pitch-black outside. It took me about twelve hours to drive to my new home. I park my motorcycle directly in front of the house. I check the time on my cell phone.

8:03 p.m.

I climb off the motorcycle, stretching my stiff limbs. It's been a while since I last stopped, so I have to take a piss. The house is yellow with white shutters. All they need is a white picket fence to qualify for the all-American family award.

I don't think we're in Kansas anymore.

I walk up the porch steps, then knock on the front door. Ricky answers with a wide smile on his face. I can tell he's nervous and the smile is forced. He knows he has a ticking time bomb on his hands now, and he has no idea when it'll go off.

"Hi, Art, how was the ride over? I was a little surprised when your mom told me you'd be riding your motorcycle here."

"It was fine. Is your plan to play Dr. Phil and try to fix me? Unfortunately, for you to accomplish that, you'll need superglue, tape, a needle and thread, and a bunch of other shit to put me back together again. The only thing that could help me is not remembering."

"I'm not trying to put you back together again. Only you can do that. That's a battle going on inside your mind. It'll take a very long time, and it's going to be really tough to win that battle. Hell, you may lose, but no matter what, I'll always be here for you. I'll be a listening ear if you need someone to talk to."

He's so fucking sincere, but I don't want his help. "You're breaking my black heart," I say sarcastically. "Are you going to let me in? I have to take a piss. Or should I just go all over your porch?"

"Oh right, sorry." He steps to the side, allowing me to enter.

This house is a home, nothing like the mansions I grew up in. Shoes are lined up beside the door. Family photos adorn the walls. The burgundy-colored furniture set is worn and matches the curtains. A jacket is draped across the back of the loveseat. Magazines cover the coffee table in front of the wide-screen television.

"Follow me. The bathroom is just before the bedroom you'll be sleeping in. The kitchen is down the hall from your bedroom, so it'll be convenient for you if you want a late-night snack or drink. All of your stuff arrived this morning…"

Now he's rambling.

"Just breathe," I say.

I walk into the bathroom, then slam the door shut. After washing my hands, I open the door and find Ricky standing there with some woman. She's a beauty with mahogany-colored skin, deep chestnut-colored eyes, and short curly black hair.

Here comes the welcoming committee.

"I'd like you to meet my girlfriend, Missy."

"It's nice to meet you, Art. Can I call you Art? I was told that's what you prefer to be called."

"Our bedroom is to the left upstairs," Ricky says.

"Wait, she lives here?"

"Yes, and her daughter too."

"Ricky, don't you know it's a sin to shack up? Missy, what type of role model are you being for your daughter?" I ask, shaking my head.

"I don't know exactly what you're used to, Art, but I can imagine. In this household, you will show respect," Ricky says.

"What did I do?" I ask innocently.

"You know damn well what you did," Ricky snaps.

"Ricky, it's fine." Missy grips his forearm. "Why don't you go get the kids so we can eat dinner? Art, you can take a look around in your bedroom. It's just down that hall."

I turn away from a seething Ricky to walk towards my temporary cage.

Cin

"If that fucker gives you any problems, you let me know. I'll be over there in a heartbeat," Trevor says.

I'm sitting cross-legged in the middle of my twin-sized bed, having a Facetime conversation with Trevor. My cousin, Lilah, is standing at the window like a lost puppy waiting on her master to come home. When she found out about Art, she invited herself to dinner. She loves fucked-up bad boys. He'll most likely be drooling all over her as soon as they meet. She's the complete opposite of me. She's super girly with enough ass and titties for the both of us. Her jeans fit like a second skin, and her ample-sized breasts are practically spilling out of her tight black V-neck sweater. Her curly hair is in a ponytail. It's going on eight o'clock, but we still haven't had dinner because my mom said we had to wait for the guest of honor to make an appearance. She has been in the kitchen for several hours, alone, insisting she cook the meal by herself. I'm very afraid.

"Don't worry."

"Josh told me all about that sick bastard."

"Trevor, I can take care of myself."

"I don't want you to take care of yourself. That's what you have me for."

"Lilah, will you move away from the damn window?"

She waves me off without looking back.

"Okay, big macho man, I'll play the damsel in distress and call on my prince if the dragon tries to slay me."

"Good. Are you leaving the window open for me tonight?"

Trevor climbs up the trellis to my window for a night time romp on occasion. He has a strong sexual appetite. I was a virgin when we started dating almost three years ago. Of course, he was not.

"I don't know. I'm a little tired," I tease.

"Come on, babe, you're killing me," he complains.

"I'll leave it open for you, you big baby." I laugh.

I hear the rumble of an engine in the distance. Lilah starts jumping up and down.

"He's here! He's here! He's riding a motorcycle. Oh my God, that's sexy as fuck."

"He's not an A-list celebrity, so calm down. I'll see you later, babe," I say.

"Okay, wear the lacy red thong I bought you," Trevor says.

I roll my eyes. "Okay, hound dog."

Trevor starts to howl, and I laugh.

"Later, babe," he says.

Leaving the bed, I'm curious to see what has Lilah's panties in a bunch. As I stand behind her, the figure leaves the motorcycle and walks up the porch steps.

"Damn, he looks good enough to eat," Lilah whispers.

She's a hot mess.

Lilah grabs her titties to push them up more.

"Hey, any more of that and your nipples will be showing," I tell her.

"Just when I thought the school year couldn't get any better," she says.

"I better go tell Josh he's here. I'll be back."

"I don't see why I have to spend my Saturday night at home because of him. I should be with my friends," Josh grumbles.

Josh sits to my right while Lilah sits across from me at the table.

"Be quiet before he hears you," Ricky whispers.

"I don't care if he does hear me."

When my mom clears her throat, we all glance at the entrance to the dining room. He's not at all what I was expecting. His hair is disheveled, but in a sexy kind of way. He has a nose and lip ring as well as pierced ears. To top off his bad-boy persona, he has a tattoo of flames dancing up his arm to end just below his ear. His black jeans hang low on his hips, and the white T-shirt exhibits his lean but taut muscular arms and chest. Where Ricky's eyes are dark green, Art's are a light clear green. He's a bit taller than Josh.

Lilah jumps out of the chair, nearly knocking it over when her eyes land on Art.

"Hi, I'm Lilah. It's nice to meet you," she says.

She can barely control her eagerness. She holds out her hand in greeting, but he doesn't take it. Instead, he looks at her hand like it's a piece of dog doo-doo. She drops her arm to her side.

"Where do you fit in this big, happy family?"

I see a flash of silver on his tongue as he talks. *He has a tongue ring.* He's full of surprises.

"Missy is my aunt. We're all happy to have you here. I'm free to show you around town, and when school starts, I'll be your personal tour guide."

Give me a fucking break. I take a drink of my water.

"Nice rack," Art says.

Water spurts from my mouth as I cough uncontrollably. Josh pats my back to help me out.

"Art," Ricky warns.

"Thank you," Lilah gushes.

"She's the one showing the girls."

Poor thing doesn't realize the comment for the insult it is. My coughing subsides.

"He'll fuck her by the end of the week," Josh says for my ears only.

"I say he'll fuck her in a few hours," I whisper.

"What the fuck did you do to your face?" Josh asks Art.

And here we go. I have a feeling it will not be peaceful in this house for the remainder of the school year.

"Jealous?"

"Fuck, no."

"Let's have a peaceful family dinner," Ricky says.

"That entire bedroom can fit inside my closet at home," Art says.

"Dad, do you want to give up your master bedroom for the king over here?"

Ricky slams his palm down on the table. Art and Josh give each other death glares.

Art moves slowly past Lilah to take a seat across from Josh, resuming their staring match. Lilah happily sits next to Art.

"This is my daughter, Cin," Mom says.

"What type of stupid ass name is that?"

"It's short for Cinnamon," I snap.

"You're named after a spice. It must suck to be you," he replies.

"It must suck—"

"I cooked a special dinner for you, chicken Marsala. I hope you like it." My mom attempts to break the tension in the dining room.

Lilah reaches for the bowl of rice, then the chicken, to serve Art a large portion. "Since you're the guest of honor, you should be served first, of course," Lilah gushes.

I'm going to be physically ill.

He puts a forkful in his mouth, then immediately spits it out.

"I wouldn't feed this crap to a pig." He brings his face to the plate and sniffs. "It looks like vomit and smells like shit."

By my mom's facial expression, I know she's crushed.

I stand, pissed on my mom's behalf. "You don't have to be so mean."

His gaze leisurely travels over my body with disgust written all over his face. "I see your cousin was blessed with all the titties and ass in the family. If you cut your hair, you could pass for a boy."

"That's enough, Art," Ricky says.

"It's not nearly enough," Art replies.

I pick up my glass and throw the remainder of the water in his face.

"Cin," Mom admonishes.

"He deserved it," I say.

I'm surprised when I feel cold water hit my face. Even though I threw my drink at him first, I wasn't expecting him to retaliate. I grab a handful of chicken Marsala and throw it at him, but he dodges out of the way and it splatters on the wall behind him. He snatches the bowl from the table and collects a handful of his own before launching it at me. I'm not as quick as him, so my face ends up covered with tonight's dinner.

"*Seu filho da puta!*" I shout.

"An eye for an eye." He smirks.

"Art, go to your room," Ricky tells him.

"Go to my room? That's rich." He laughs.

"I mean it." Ricky puts on his best stern face.

"Where I'm going is to get a decent meal," he replies.

"Wait, I can go with you and show you where all the good spots are," Lilah offers, standing.

He doesn't acknowledge her as he leaves the dining room. She sits back down, dejected.

"Nice going, Dad. You brought that asshole into our house, though he isn't lying about the chicken Marsala. I don't want to hurt your feelings, Missy, but it's awful."

"Sorry, I'll order some pizza," she says in a defeated voice.

"I'm going to go clean myself up," I mutter, feeling foolish.

Well, that was a great introduction. One point for Art. Zero for Cin.

CHAPTER six

I travel down the road at eighty miles per hour. They must fucking hate me now, which means this living arrangement won't last too long. I wouldn't be surprised if my uncle sent me packing when I get back. I didn't go in there with the intention to royally fuck this up, but I couldn't control myself. Lilah is going to be an issue. She basically gave me an invitation tonight, but sex hasn't been a part of my existence for a long time. I'm a teenage boy, so of course it crosses my mind, but I haven't had the urge to follow through. I lost my virginity at age thirteen to a twenty-seven-year-old who frequents the same social circles as my mother. I may be young, but I'm no stranger in the art of pleasing the female body.

Though I have no interest in Lilah, *Cin* is a different matter. When I entered the dining room, I saw her as another forgettable teenage girl. There was nothing special about her. Though she's not ugly, she's no beauty queen. When she threw her glass of water in my face, my attention shifted to really take in her appearance. The fire in her eyes along with the rapid rise and fall of her chest in anger was sexy as fuck. The icing on the cake is her shiny dark hip-length hair with pink highlights, inviting pouty lips, clear creamy skin, and mesmerizing russet-colored eyes. She wore no bra, so I could see the outline of her nipples through her thin T-shirt. Her name suits her… *Cin*. I felt a spark, and as insignificant as it was, it caused life to breathe into my heart. Adrenaline coursed through my veins, increasing the flow of blood. The feeling is welcome but unwelcome at the same time. I want to continue the battle of wills with her. She's going to be an issue, but for a different reason.

I hear police sirens behind me.

Shit, just what I fucking need.

I do not need to be on the cops' radar my first day in town. I pull my motorcycle to a stop on the side of the road. I turn off the engine and release the kickstand. I peer back, watching the cop leave his cruiser to make his way towards me.

"Get off the motorcycle, son."

"I'm not your son," I reply, doing as he says.

"You were going eighty in a fifty. That's foolish and reckless. Are you trying to get yourself killed?"

Yes. "I didn't notice the speed limit."

"Are you new in town?"

"Yep. It's my first day, to be exact."

"Visiting?"

"I'm staying with my uncle until the end of the school year."

"You Ricky's nephew?"

Good ole Ricky already warned the law around these parts about me.

"I am."

"I'm Sheriff Andy Livingston. Since Ricky is a good friend of mine, I'll let you off with a warning, but I still need to see your license and registration."

He takes the offered documents and heads back to his cruiser. After a few minutes, he's back at my side.

"Stay out of trouble," he says in a serious tone.

"Sure thing, Sheriff. Do you know where I can get something to eat around here?"

"Judy's has the best damn cheeseburgers in town. Breakfast is served all day too, if that's your fancy. Keep going straight until you hit Division, then turn left at the stop sign. The diner will be on your right."

"Thanks."

"You're welcome. Remember what I said."

"Will do," I say, continuing on my way.

I enter the diner a short time later.

"Have a seat anywhere you like, darlin'," a curvy redhead tells me from behind the counter. The diner is a little crowded, being it's a Saturday night and all. I sit at the last booth in the back to be incognito.

"Hello, my name is Mandy. I'll be your server tonight. What can I get for you?" She's a cute blond, around my age. I wonder if she attends the high school I'll be starting next week.

"I'll have the famous cheeseburger I've heard about."

"Excellent choice. How would you like that cooked?"

"Medium rare."

"Fries with that?"

"Yeah, and a Pepsi."

"You new around here?"

"I am."

"Guess you'll be attending Central High."

"That's the plan."

"Maybe I'll see you around," she says, flirting.

"That's a possibility."

Another girl I'll need to stay clear of.

She walks off with a come-hither smile on her face. I'm sipping my Pepsi when a group of boys walks in. My senses are instantly on alert. Trouble recognizes trouble. The guy in front must be the ringleader, and his eyes land on me. When they move towards me, I'm ready. Ringleader places his palms flat on the table, leaning towards me. The look of him screams jock, like Josh—tall with an athlete's physique. His dirty-blond–colored hair falls slightly below his ears.

"I'm assuming you're new around here, so I'll give you a pass this one time. This is our table. Move," Ringleader says.

"That's funny. I don't see a name anywhere on it."

There are four against one, but still I'll take my chances. Though, most likely, I'll be taking an ass whooping tonight. His eyebrows lift in surprise over his sable-colored eyes. He expected me to scramble out of the booth, but I don't intimidate easily. I'm not the fucking one. Number One and Number Two move in closer. I'm guessing they're brothers, since they have the same pale-blue eyes and auburn hair color.

"Danny, don't start no shit tonight."

"Mind your business, Mandy, and get back to work. I gave this *boy* a warning. It's not my problem if he didn't listen." He doesn't take his eyes off me while talking to Mandy.

"I'm going to call your daddy."

"I'm shaking in my boots." He snickers.

Mandy runs off.

"Are you sure you want to go down this route, *boy*?"

"Of course. The scenery is to die for."

I deliver a blow to Ringleader's gut before popping him in the eye when he doubles over. I push him back, then grab my drink and the ketchup bottle from the table. When Number One charges me, I jump from the booth, throwing the cup, which hits him square in the forehead. He grasps his head, falling to his knees. I break the glass ketchup bottle over Number Two's head. Customers start to scream and flee the diner, while others take out their cell phones to record. My eyes connect with Number Three's hazel ones as he takes a swing at me. I kick him in the dick, because yeah, I fight dirty. When number three hunches over to clutch his manhood, I grab him by his curly blond hair and slam his face into the table. He falls to the floor with a bloody nose. Number One recovers and wraps his arms around my midsection, tackling me into the wall. I'm elbowing him in the back when Ketchup Head grabs my arm and pins it to the wall, preventing me from continuing the assault on his friend. This gives Pepsi enough time to grab my other arm and pin it against the wall too.

Ringleader stands in front of me now with Number Three next to him. I struggle against the other boys' hold.

"Keep him still," shouts Ringleader. Now, you get your ass handed to you."

He delivers blow after blow to my torso. Damn, this fucker hits hard.

"It's my turn," Number Three says.

"I guess this means we won't be painting each other's toenails and having sleepovers anytime soon," I mock.

"I'm not done yet."

"Yes, you are." It's Sheriff Andy.

"Dad, he started—" Ringleader begins.

Dad?

"Let him go now!" the sheriff shouts.

Oh fuck, I get into a fight with this bastard after his father warned me less than an hour ago to stay out of trouble.

The assholes drop my arms. Fuck me, my body hurts.

"I knew you were trouble when I first saw you." The sheriff shakes his head.

"Now, Sheriff, I saw the whole thing. Your son came in here looking for trouble and he found it," the curvy redhead says in my defense.

It seems as if he doesn't believe her.

"I saw what happened too, and Danny started the fight," Mandy chimes in.

"You and your friends go home, Danny," the sheriff says.

Danny and his bozos leave.

"I'll be stopping by to speak with your uncle in a few."

Fucking terrific.

"Go home," the sheriff says.

"I haven't eaten dinner yet."

"I don't give a damn."

I figure I've caused enough havoc for one night, so I leave, but not to go back to Ricky's. I need dinner first.

CHAPTER seven

ART

It's just after midnight when I arrive back at the house. Damn, I don't have a key and all the lights are off. At least my uncle is asleep. I don't feel like dealing with his bullshit. Maybe the front door was left unlocked for me. I twist the doorknob and push.

Thank God for small favors. I step inside then close it as quietly as I can. *Home free.* When I turn from the door, a light is switched on.

Fuck.

Ricky is leaning against the banister.

"Where have you been?"

"Out," I answer nonchalantly.

"There are rules here. You can't do whatever you want."

"Well, that's a problem for me because I like breaking rules," I say mockingly.

His jaw clenches. He's losing patience quickly.

"Sheriff Andy came by earlier."

"And just what did the good ole sheriff have to say?"

"You were speeding, and you got into a fight with a group of boys."

"I was defending myself. Every American has the right to defend themselves."

I'm done talking. I move to walk by him, but he grabs my arm to stop my progress.

I snatch my arm back. "Don't you ever touch me again."

"Art, I'm not the enemy."

"Are you my savior then?"

"I want to help."

"It's too late for that."

"Give this a chance."

"I can't be helped!" I shout.

"That day I found you—"

"Where were you? When I woke up in the hospital, you were gone. If you cared so much… If you wanted to help me… Where the fuck did you go?"

"Your mother was in no shape to make any decisions at that time. She gave that right to my father. He prevented me from visiting you. My hands were tied. There was nothing I could do."

"You could've tried harder."

"I'm sorry I failed you, but I'm here now. Don't let this be the end of the road. You have the rest of your life ahead of you."

"My life ended the night Cole's did."

He doesn't stop me a second time when I walk past him.

Cin

"Trevor, you have to leave," I say.

I gently nudge him on the shoulder to wake him up. His big body takes up most of my bed.

"I don't want to go," he grumbles.

"You have to before morning." I smile, straddling his hips.

"One more time before I go."

He brings my lips to his for a passionate kiss. I grip the base of his dick, guiding him into my pussy. Once I'm completely filled, I begin to rock my hips back and forth at a steady pace. My pussy is sore since we've fucked several times now. Trevor groans and deepens our kiss. Josh knows about Trevor's nighttime visits, but he gets pissed if he hears us, so I try to keep as quiet as possible. As I feel my orgasm building, I increase my speed. Trevor grips my ass to hold me still so he can take over the pace of our fucking. He thrusts his hips upwards in a frantic motion. My pussy clenches as I climax. He slams into me until he finds his own release.

"*Eu te amo*," I whisper against his ear.

"I love you too," he replies gruffly.

He rolls me under him and runs kisses along my collarbone.

"I want to stay for a few more hours."

"No." I swat him on the butt. "You have to go." I laugh.

"Fine. Come over for dinner and a movie tomorrow night," he says.

"Is your mom cooking her famous meatloaf, mashed potatoes, and green beans? If she is, I'll be there with bells on."

"I'll make that request just for you."

He pulls his softening dick out of me and leaves the bed to dress. I roll to my side to watch him, my head resting on my upturned hand.

"See you later, babe," he says.

"Okay."

He pecks my lips before moving my thick purple curtains to the side to climb out the window and down the trellis.

I leave my bed and put on my panties and T-shirt, then head downstairs for a bottled water.

As I approach the kitchen, I hear a noise coming from the hall leading to Art's bedroom. Curiosity gets the best of me, and I change directions. I see light shining from underneath the door.

Art must still be awake.

My steps falter. Do I really want to poke the bear?

"Cole, I'm coming! Don't give up! Stay above the water."

He's having a nightmare.

"Cole, I'm so sorry... so sorry. I should've been there for you."

His voice is filled with sorrow. I lightly knock on the door.

"Art, are you okay?"

No answer.

I twist the doorknob and push. I slowly walk towards Art as he thrashes in the middle of the bed, drenched in sweat, with only boxer briefs hiding his nudity. I take in the tattoo on his chest. I wonder how many tattoos he has. As I move closer, I see cuts covering his hard abs, some fresh blood still seeping from them. On the nightstand, there's a razor covered in blood. It takes me a few seconds to process the scene before me.

Art's a cutter.

I move closer to stand directly over the bed. I should leave, but I can't. His cheeks are wet with tears. I run my fingers over the puckered skin of the healed wounds. His eyes snap open. His hand moves quick as lightning, clasping onto my wrist. Anger transforms his facial features. He yanks me forward, causing me to tumble onto the bed. He rolls over and pins me under his big body, then latches his strong hand around my throat.

"What the fuck are you doing in here?" he sneers in my face. He's wild with fury. "Don't you ever come in my bedroom again, or I'll make you squeal. Do you understand me?" he yells.

I claw at his hand in an effort to get him to release me. I can't breathe.

I'm going to die.

His grip on my throat tightens. I see blackness at the edge of my vision. I panic and vigorously thrash against his hold. I can feel his dick getting hard.

What the fuck?

He closes his eyes and shivers. When they open again, a new emotion manifests in their depths.

Unbridled lust.

He pushes my thighs open with his knee to rest between them. He grinds his stiff dick against the thin fabric of my panties. I feel like the worst girlfriend in the world because *damn,* I fucking love the feel of his dick rubbing against my slick heat. The friction causes my sensitive pussy to throb greedily, wanting to feel him inside. I like what this demented boy is doing to me. He latches onto my bottom lip, biting down hard. His hand around my throat prevents me from screaming.

Tears roll down the side of my face as the coppery taste of blood fills my mouth.

"Come in here again, I'm going to spread you wide and fuck the shit out of you. It won't be a gentle fucking for you. No, I'm going to split you the fuck open and make you bleed."

He throws me off the bed. I land on my head, so it takes me a few seconds to come to my senses. I cough, struggling to take deep breaths.

"You have three seconds to get out of here. If you're still here when I'm done counting, I'm going to take it as an invitation that you want to fuck."

I start to crawl to the door.

"One."

I try to move faster.

"Two."

He leaves the bed and begins to trail me. I make it out the door, turning to rest against the wall. My T-shirt is stained with his blood. My body is trembling, and it's still very difficult to breathe. My gaze travels from his toned legs to his bulging manhood, clearly visible through his boxer briefs, then over his taut stomach and muscular chest and finally connects with his eyes. I wipe the blood dripping from the side of my mouth with a shaky hand.

If looks could kill...

He slams the door shut. Once I am able to stand, I run upstairs back to my room, forgetting all about the bottled water needed to quench my thirst.

CHAPTER eight

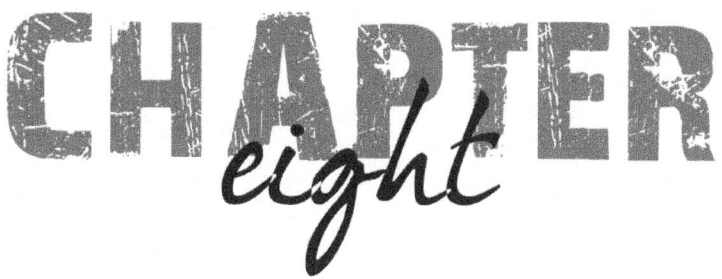

ART

I lie on my temporary bed, staring at the ceiling. In a few hours, it'll be a new year.

Another year without Cole.

It's been two days since I woke up to Cin standing over me. She knows my secret now, but surprisingly, she hasn't told anyone. I was sure my uncle was going to come barreling into my bedroom to ship me off to a mental institution that night, but it never happened. Her sweet, warm flesh is more addicting than cocaine. The feel of her beneath me won't leave my mind. Her pussy was on fire, the heat enveloping my dick. I haven't felt the urge to fuck in a very long time, but my God. That night, I wanted to fuck us both into oblivion. Now there are three things constantly beating at my mind: Cole, cocaine, and *Cin*.

I've jerked off a few times with thoughts of my dick pounding through her tight little pussy. One thing's for certain, *I want to live in Cin.* She tries her best to stay away from me, but that's not always possible. When we happen to end up in a room alone, she dashes to the exit. It's the complete opposite for me. My gaze continues to seek her out. I hate myself for it, but I don't have control. It's the only reason I eat dinner in the dining room with everyone else, not because my uncle demands it. I always deliberately sit next to her, but she doesn't glance my way. Watching her squirm makes my dick hard.

My cousin, on the other hand, shoulder-checks me whenever we cross paths. It's cool, because I shoulder-check his bitch ass right back. If he swings on me, that's when the real trouble will start.

I leave my room in search of something to drink. When I enter the kitchen, my cousin is leaning against the counter drinking a Sprite. He glares at me.

"You have something you want to say to me?" I ask.

"Yeah, leave."

Ricky walks into the kitchen.

"Good, just the two guys I want to speak to. Missy and I are going to be heading out in about an hour. What do you plan on doing tonight, Josh?"

"Cin and I are going to hang with the crew."

"Okay, I want you to take Art along."

"That's not going to happen."

I don't like the idea of ringing in the new year with him or his asshole friends either, but since Cin is going, so will I. The bonus is I know it'll piss Josh off if I tag along.

"I wasn't asking, Josh."

"Thank you for the invite, Josh. It warms my heart that you're so welcoming. What time do we leave?"

"If he doesn't go, no one goes," Ricky says.

"Fine," Josh mutters.

"Well, that's settled then. Have a good night, boys." Ricky leaves the kitchen.

"We leave at eleven. Be ready, or you get left."

I salute him before grabbing a Coke out of the refrigerator before leaving the kitchen.

"Prick," he mumbles.

Cin

I descend the stairs with Trevor's arms wrapped around my stomach with his lips at my neck.

"Keep your hands to yourself." I smile.

"But I'd rather keep them all over you," he whispers in my ear.

My smile slips when I see Art sitting on the coffee table. Josh is waiting by the front door.

"What is he doing here?" Trevor asks.

Art smirks while his eyes stare daggers at Trevor. I'm unnerved about Art and Trevor being in such close proximity after the intimate moment we shared the other day. I'm on alert whenever he's around. As fucked up as it sounds, my body is aware of him. I barely know this boy, but I want to give him a hug and offer comfort. I must be insane to think that way about him after the way he treated me.

"He's coming with us?" I ask, astonished.

"Yep," Josh answers. "You can thank my father for that."

Trevor moves around me to size Art up.

I assumed he would rather be hit by a tractor trailer than hang out with Josh.

"Can he be trusted to keep his mouth shut?" Trevor asks.

"Absolutely not," Josh replies.

"We can't risk bringing him with us," Trevor states.

"I have no choice. Either he goes, or we all stay in."

"I can speak for my fucking self," Art says. "Do I look like a little bitch who's going to run with my tail between my legs to the authorities? I don't give a fuck what you hillbillies do."

"Who you calling hillbilly, nut job?" Josh sneers.

As Josh moves in Art's direction, he stands from the coffee table, ready for whatever is about to pop off. Josh stops only when he's in Art's personal space. Trevor leaves my side to stand next to Josh.

Fuck. If they start fighting, I won't be able to break them up on my own.

"If you're feeling froggy, leap, motherfucker," Art mocks. His hands form fists at his sides. He's itching for a fight.

I walk swiftly over to situate myself between the cousins. Tempers are rising quickly.

I place my palms on their chests to hold them at bay. Even through Art's shirt, I swear I felt a current travel up my arm the moment my hand touches him. When my gaze catches his, I know he felt it too.

"This isn't happening. We need to go. You two can measure dicks later," I say.

After a few gut-wrenching minutes, Josh speaks first. "You're about to enter Chaos," he says in an ominous tone.

"What?"

"The Nine Months of Chaos, to be exact," Trevor says.

"Stop speaking in fucking riddles."

"It's a rite of passage you're intruding on. The "in" crowd of the graduating class causes havoc for the poor citizens of Longhorn County from September until graduation," Trevor explains.

Josh cuts in. "During Chaos, if you're not out of control, you're not in control."

"What's the plan tonight?" Art asks in an I-don't-give-a-shit voice.

"We're going to McKinley High in the next county to fuck up their school. They're our number one rival," Josh answers.

"Oh wow, you guys love living dangerously," Art replies sarcastically.

Josh shoots Art a death glare as his cell phone rings.

"Hello? Yeah, it's time for Chaos."

He ends the phone call.

"They're heading to the school. Let's go." Josh walks towards the door.

He picks up the bag filled with orange and green spray paint and a drill sitting by the front door. Green and orange are our school colors, so officials will know kids from Central did the damage, but they won't know who.

Art walks towards his motorcycle when we leave the house. Josh looks over at him with a frown on his face.

"Where the fuck are you going?" Josh asks.

"I'll follow behind you."

"No, you won't. You have to ride with us," Josh tells him.

"Fuck that."

"Asshole, you can't ride your motorcycle. That thing is loud as fuck. It'll be like having a target on your back. We need to be discreet."

"Fine," he agrees.

Trevor and I climb into the back of Josh's dark-gray Chevy Suburban while Art gets in the front.

CHAPTER nine

Cin

Josh drives around to the back of the large building, then parks his truck between Danny's Ford Mustang and Aiden's Nissan Armada. When Josh kills the engine, everyone exits the vehicles. The whole crew is here.

"Motherfucker!" Danny shouts.

Everyone is instantly on alert, peering around to find out what has Danny riled.

He rushes Art, tackling him to the ground.

"Danny, what the fuck?" Josh looks on in confusion.

Art gains the upper hand by pinning Danny under him. Danny unsuccessfully tries to dislodge him. Blood pours from his mouth as Art relentlessly pummels his face.

Bri, Lilah, and Anneli move to stand beside Trevor and me.

"My lips just quivered, and I don't mean the ones on my face." Bri licks her lips.

"Back off, bitch, he's mine," Lilah hisses.

"Here we go again," Anneli groans.

Anneli has beautiful kinky hair with milk chocolate-colored skin and eyes. She's a little taller than me, with an ass most women would need surgery to achieve. She's on the track and field team too. Zeke's totally in love with her. I'm always telling her to give him a chance. Too bad for him, her response is always the same: "I don't date guys with jock syndrome." Whatever that means.

"All's fair in love and war," Bri replies.

Lilah and Bri pretty much have the same body type. The only difference is Bri's dyed platinum-blond, chin-length curls and expressive amber eyes. This won't be the first or last time they go after the same guy. At one time, they were fighting over Danny, but he never had any intentions of going steady with either of them. He only wanted sex. They're both on the cheerleading team, but Bri made captain. She uses every opportunity to shove that fact in Lilah's face.

"That's the bastard who broke a ketchup bottle over my head," Aiden growls.

"He do that to your nose, Zeke?" Dex pops his gum.

"Fuck you, man."

"Hey, it's not my fault you got your ass kicked." Dex smirks as he pushes his glasses up the bridge of his nose.

Robbie kicks Art in the face, finally displacing him from Danny's chest. Art lets out a loud grunt as his body makes contact with the concrete. Robbie moves to kick Art again, but he swiftly rolls over to avoid being struck, throwing out his leg to connect with Robbie's stomach. Art lumbers to his feet.

"Son of a bitch," Robbie hisses.

"Josh, do something." I start to panic. They could really hurt Art. It's hardly fair with four against one.

Josh stares at me with an unreadable expression on his face. "It's time for Chaos."

Danny, Aiden, Robbie, and Zeke surround him.

"Bring it on, bitches." Art rotates his shoulders.

"This should be interesting." Dex grins.

Dex's shaggy hair is a bright orange-red and goes perfectly with his freckle-covered alabaster skin. He's a nerd with one hot body. He has a thing for Bri, but she never gives him the time of day. She's obsessed with the "rebel without a cause" type.

Art's not afraid, even with the odds against him. Trevor pulls me back when I move to walk towards the group to prevent the fight.

Oh fuck, it's about to go down.

"Trevor, we have to stop them." I struggle against his hold.

"Let's see how tough he really is," he responds.

When Danny swings, Art ducks, then comes up with an uppercut. Danny falls back, cracking his head on the concrete. Zeke catches an elbow to the face when he comes at Art from the right.

"Fuck! He broke my nose again!"

"My new man is a hell of a fighter," Bri gushes.

Lilah gives Bri her best "fuck off, bitch" face.

"This is not the reason why we're here. We don't have time for this shit!" Anneli yells. At least I have one person on my side.

"She's right. Stop this," I say.

Robbie takes ahold of Art's right arm while Aiden grabs his left, and they drag him over to the Mustang to hold him against the hood. Danny climbs to his feet and walks over to a struggling Art.

"Now you pay," Danny says.

"No, me first. This fucker broke my nose twice."

Zeke begins to rain punch after punch on Art's upper body.

I turn my head to look Trevor in the eyes. "Please, stop this. Please, I'm begging you."

After a few seconds, he finally says, "Josh, it's time to end this before somebody gets seriously hurt."

I sigh in relief.

Josh walks over to Zeke and wraps his forearm around his neck to pull him away from Art. "Easy, man," Josh says.

Art jerks his arms away from Robbie and Aiden.

"Stay the fuck out of this, Josh." Danny jabs a finger in Josh's direction.

"I don't like this asshole any more than you do, but he's my cousin," he replies, letting go of Zeke.

"You're related to this dipshit?" Danny exclaims.

"Yep, and I don't want to have to explain to my father how he ended up in the hospital during his first week here."

"Watch your back," Danny threatens.

"Ditto, motherfucker," Art replies.

Zeke spits a mouth full of blood at Art's feet. Art smirks in response.

I walk over to Art. "Are you okay?"

Blood drips down the corner of his mouth, but other than a few scrapes and bruises, he seems fine. "Why do you care?"

"I don't."

"Then run along back to your boyfriend. He's watching," Art mocks.

"Fucking asshole," I say, walking back over to a disgruntled Trevor.

"What did you say to him?" Trevor asks.

"I just wanted to see if he's okay."

"He's trouble. I know it's impossible for you to avoid him entirely since you live in the same house, but don't seek him out."

He kisses my forehead when I nod in understanding.

"I say Josh's cousin won the fight." Dex scratches his head.

"Shut the fuck up, Dex, before I break your glasses," Zeke grumbles as he attempts to stop the flow of blood with the hem of his shirt.

"Dex, stop provoking them," Trevor says.

"How the fuck did the four of you get beat up by one person?" Dex asks, causing Danny to punch him in the stomach.

"Ouch." Dex rubs the abused area.

"Can we finally do what we came here for, please?" Anneli asks in annoyance. She's the no-nonsense one of the group and has had it with their bullshit.

Dex takes his laptop out of his carrying case and places it on the hood of the Mustang. "Watch me work my magic," he says.

He cracks his knuckles before getting to work. Dex is a phenomenal hacker. His job for tonight is to disable McKinley's alarm system and video feed so there's no evidence of who vandalized the school. Once it's clear, Josh will use a drill to get through the lock.

"Zeke, do you have the mice?" Josh asks.

"Yeah, I've been catching these little motherfuckers in the barn for the last few weeks. I have a big tub filled with them in the truck."

"And I have the liquid skunk essence," Danny says. He unscrews the top and takes a whiff. "This shit smells like donkey ass."

Bri walks over to Art and attempts to engage in conversation with him, but his attention is on me. It's unnerving. She struts in front of him, flirting outrageously while flipping her hair. Lilah looks like she wants to bite her head off.

"Hurry the hell up, Dex. We don't have all night," Robbie complains.

"You can't rush awesomeness." Dex smiles.

"Speed it up, Dex," Josh demands.

"Done. It's time for Chaos," Dex announces.

"Okay, let's go," Robbie says.

The group moves towards the entrance. I look back at Art before I realize what I'm doing. Lilah and Bri are on either side of him, vying for his attention.

Josh pushes the door open once he successfully drills through the lock.

"All right, let's get this show on the road," Robbie says.

I give Bri, Lilah, and Anneli a can of spray paint. "It's a bit dull in here ladies, don't you agree? How about we add a little color?"

"You three are on mice duty." Josh points at Danny, Zeke, and Aiden. "You two are on stink duty with me," he tells Trevor and Robbie. "I want this place smelling like rotten ass. Dex, you're our lookout."

"Come on. I want some Chaos too," Dex complains.

"Next time, man."

"I don't give a fuck what you do," Josh says to Art, walking by him.

Danny runs down the hall. "Yeah, baby! Let's cause some Chaos!"

We disperse to complete our assigned tasks.

CHAPTER ten

ART

After making Chaos for an hour, we leave the school. It must be nice to be a normal teenager, doing normal teenager shit. I can't relate to them. In another lifetime, they could've been my friends. I would've participated in the merriment of Chaos, taking shots to bring in the new year with them.

Fuck, I don't belong here.

I'm a fool to chase Cin, but I'm drawn to her. I can't explain why. I don't care that she has a boyfriend. I still want a taste. As I watch her with that asshole Trevor, I experience a whole new emotion—one I've never felt before.

Envy.

Mix in guilt, hate, and grief—all of these emotions create an unstable bomb within me that can go off at any moment.

"You two do realize you're not alone, right?" Josh smirks.

I watch them through the mirror on the drive back to the house. Trevor's kissing her neck, her face, her lips... I wish it were my lips running along her soft skin. I want to reach back and pull them apart. I immediately leave the truck when Josh comes to a stop in front of the house before I do something I'll regret.

"What the fuck is his problem?" I hear Trevor ask.

"Who cares?" Josh replies.

My uncle gave me a key, so I'm able to go inside the house without having to wait on my asshole cousin. I enter my bedroom, slam the door shut, and pace like a caged lion, feeling agitated and volatile. Maybe I should go pick a fight with Josh. After a few minutes, I hear a light knock.

I'm surprised to find Cin standing there when I open the door.

"What the fuck do you want? I told you what would happen the next time you came in here."

Her mouth opens to reply, but no words come out. I move until my lips are at her ear, my body brushing against hers. Her hair smells so fucking good, like sweet strawberries. I wonder if that's how her pussy will taste.

"Is that what you came here for? Are you ready for me to fuck you?" I ask in a low voice.

I don't want to be her boyfriend. I wouldn't know how. But I do want to fuck her, and fuck her I will. When I'm done, I'll give what's left of her back to her bitch ass boyfriend. I place a kiss just below her earlobe. She moans before stepping back. My first instinct is to grab her, to pull her forward, but before I can, she holds up a little square box. It's a first aid kit. I hadn't realized she was holding it at her side.

"I came to clean your cuts," she replies softly.

"Where's your boyfriend?"

"He went home."

I step to the side, allowing her entry before closing the door. Her progress stops when she reaches the middle of the room. Even in her loose-fitting jeans and plain red T-shirt, she's sexy as fuck. I walk by her to sit on the edge of the bed. She doesn't move or talk. She simply stands there.

"Well? What are you waiting for?" I ask.

Cin slowly moves towards me, like an animal catcher approaching a rabid dog. She puts the first aid kit on the bed beside me before opening it to take out alcohol pads.

She gasps as I pull her between my spread legs.

"I'm waiting, nurse."

I keep my hands on her waist. She tears open the little packet to retrieve the alcohol pad, then carefully goes over the cuts on my face.

"You're a cutter," she states.

"What's your point?"

"Why do you do it?"

"It helps me to cope."

"With what happened to your brother?"

I nod. I've never opened up to anyone, not even my therapist. I don't know what makes her special. I barely know her. After she finishes cleaning the cuts on my face, she covers them with ointment.

"Does it help?"

"A little."

"Have you thought about getting help?"

"The only thing that can help me is a time machine. Why didn't you tell anyone?" I ask her.

She lifts my right hand from her hip to clean my bruised knuckles, then applies ointment before answering. "It's not my secret to tell."

"Why are you here?" I ask, my eyes boring into hers.

"I don't know," she whispers.

"I know why."

I pull her T-shirt up to expose her flat stomach. Fuck, she has a belly button piercing. The dangling gold bird contrasts beautifully with her skin tone. She yanks my head closer, moaning loudly when my tongue dips into her navel before trailing kisses along the soft warm flesh. Her skin quivers beneath my lips. She sways on her feet as her breathing becomes labored. I unbutton her jeans, then tug them down to expose her purple panties. My kisses travel to her pussy. She glides her fingers through my hair when I latch onto her cotton-covered clit. My hand slides under her panties to grip her bare ass, stopping her from falling when her legs buckle. The moans leaving her mouth are like music to my ears.

"Stop, this isn't right. I can't do this."

"Nah, there's no stopping now."

She staggers back, breaking my hold on her before jerking her jeans back up. She turns to flee, but I'm right behind her. She pulls the door open to make good on her escape, but it's too late. I slam it shut and press into her back. I twist my hand in her long hair, pushing the side of her face into the door.

"You're hurting me."

"You knew what would happen if you came in here again. You were warned," I whisper in her ear.

"Let me go."

"It's too late for that now."

I push my hand into her panties to circle her clit with the pad of my finger.

"Tell me you don't like it, but we both know it won't be the truth."

She whimpers when I move my hand lower to dip into her slit. I grind my hard dick against her.

"Your pussy wouldn't be this wet if you weren't ready for my dick."

I bring my hand to my nose to sniff. "Mmm. Strawberries."

I smear her wetness on the side of her neck before covering the area with my mouth to suck deeply. I push down her jeans and panties, then I undo my zipper and free my dick through the opening. I detangle my hand from her hair to hoist her up, making it easier to position myself at her entrance. I begin to push forward, penetrating her tightness.

"This isn't right." Tears roll down her cheeks.

I'm at war with myself because, fuck, I don't want to stop. I should keep going. She provoked me, tempted me. She knew what the fuck she was doing when she knocked on my bedroom door. I lower her to the floor and step back. She rights her clothes, then grasps the doorknob. I place my palm on the door before she can open it.

"I swear on my brother, if you even glance in the direction of my bedroom again, this is happening, and more than the tip of my dick will be tunneling through your tight pussy. You can scream, cry, fight, do whatever the fuck you want, but I won't stop until my cum is dripping from your cunt. You don't poke the fucking bear during hibernation and not expect to be mauled when he wakes."

With my threat hanging between us, I remove my palm to let her run from my bedroom.

Cin

Giving up on sleep, I finally leave my bedroom in frustration for a run before school starts. My thoughts are a jumbled mess as I jog down the road. I left for Trevor's house early in the morning on New Year's Day because I didn't want to face Art. Though I spent the whole day there, my mind kept drifting back to him.

I'm the worst kind of girlfriend.

The moment Art's lips touched my stomach, I could barely stand, lost in sensations I'd never felt before. Art saw right through my bullshit. He knew why I came knocking on his door, while I was in denial. Why am I drawn to someone as damaged as he is? He's a puzzle with missing pieces.

Guilt is what stopped me that night. I wanted him… I wanted him bad. The night I invaded his privacy by going into his bedroom without being invited connected us somehow. I witnessed him at his worst, when he was most vulnerable. Part of me was hoping he wouldn't stop so I could lay the blame solely at his feet. When I felt the pressure of his dick opening me up, the reality of what I was about to do hit me like a ton of bricks. The need to feel him inside me and my loyalty to Trevor battled for supremacy. After arriving home last night, I couldn't stop myself from going to Art's bedroom door, but I didn't dare go in. I listened while he cried out for his brother, and I ached for him. I went upstairs when I couldn't stand to listen to his anguished cries anymore.

I see a jogger appear on the road as I make my way back towards the house. I guess I'm not the only one who couldn't sleep. As I get closer to the lone figure, I recognize who it is.

Art.

We slow down to a walk, then come to a complete stop a few yards from each other. His intense green eyes don't waver from me.

"I couldn't sleep," I say lamely.

The sight of him does something to me. He's beautiful. I know that's not the correct word to use to describe someone as masculine as him, but that's the first word that pops into my mind when I look at him.

His thick raven hair, crystal-clear green eyes, plump pink lips…

He's. Fucking. Beautiful.

My mouth waters when he gradually resumes his progress towards me. I'm rooted to the spot. He only stops when there's no space separating us. He's at least three heads taller than me so I have to crane my head up to meet his eyes. After a few seconds, he brushes by me to continue his jog. I turn around and watch him until he disappears.

ART

Central High is definitely not like the fancy private schools I'm used to attending, I observe while waiting in the main office to have a talk with the principal. It seems my uncle has already had a conversation with him about his troublesome nephew. A tall, skinny man with snow-white hair emerges from the back. I stand as he walks over to me.

"You must be Arthur." He holds out his hand, but I don't take it.

"Art."

"Okay, Art it is. I'm Principal Taylor." He drops his arm to his side. "I figured it'd be beneficial for us to have a little chat since it's your first day. If you don't mind?"

"Actually, I do mind."

"It'll only take a few minutes, Art."

"It looks like I don't have a choice."

"I promise I won't take up too much of your time."

I follow Principal Taylor to his office. He steps to the side, motioning for me to enter first. He waves his hand in the direction of a worn discolored chair in front of a rickety desk. I drop down in the chair with unnecessary force. After closing the door, he sits in the equally outdated chair behind his desk.

"I hope you enjoyed the holidays," he says with a wide smile on his face.

"It was shitty."

My reply causes his smile to slip. "Art, I want you to finish your senior year on a positive note—"

I cut him off. "I'm not interested in this bullshit pep talk."

"Just complete all the assignments given to you, keep your head down, and stay out of trouble. It's that simple."

"You see, the problem with that is trouble always finds me, and when it comes knocking, I have to answer the door."

The expression on his face turns to one of irritation.

"Are we done here?"

When he nods, I stand, preparing to leave his damn office.

"One more thing," he says.

Now what? I let out a heavy sigh and shoot him with my best hurry-the-fuck-up look.

"A high school was vandalized sometime during the winter break. You're new in town, but I thought I'd still ask if you know anything about it?"

"I don't," I answer.

Fuck my cousin and his friends, but a snitch I'll never be.

Cin

Mr. Beck is going on and on about the curriculum and expectations when Art enters the classroom. He's wearing destroyed faded denim jeans, a shirt with some logo I'm unfamiliar with, and expensive-looking shoes. His clothes probably cost more than every student's outfit in class. My heart starts to pound in my chest. Trevor follows my line of vision.

"You've got to be fucking joking. Why the hell did he have to end up with us?" he mutters.

The bell for class rang five minutes ago, and I had breathed a sigh of relief, thankful we wouldn't be in human biology class together. I don't want him and Trevor in the same classroom. I'm afraid of what'll be said. Art is unpredictable. I hope this is the only class they have together.

"Good morning," Mr. Beck says in greeting.
"Morning."
"I'm Mr. Beck."
"Art."
"Principal Taylor already emailed me to inform me you'd be a little late. Take a seat, anywhere."

Please don't come back here.

But of course Art does. He sits a few desks down from Trevor and me. Something tells me if those desks weren't already occupied, Art would've sat next to me. I see him staring at me from the corner of my eye.

"What the fuck are you looking at?" Trevor growls.

"Your girlfriend. She looks fucking good."

Oh, no.

Trevor stands. "You want to say that again?"

I grab Trevor's wrist. "Sit down. He only wants to get a rise out of you," I whisper.

Our classmates are animatedly watching the altercation unfold.

"I don't need to. You heard what I said." Art slowly rises to his full height, without a care in the world.

When Trevor tries to snatch his wrist from my grasp, I stand, latching onto him with my other hand to pull him back. "No, Trevor, don't. Sit down and ignore him. Don't do this in school."

"You better listen to your girlfriend. I have nothing to lose, but you do."

I glare at Art.

"Is there a problem, gentleman?" Mr. Beck asks.

"No, Mr. Beck, simply a misunderstanding," Trevor answers as he sits down.

"That's what I thought," Art taunts.

Trevor stiffens, but I'm relieved when he ignores him.

The PA system clicks on. "All seniors report to the auditorium for an emergency assembly immediately."

CHAPTER twelve

ART

I notice Sheriff Andy sitting in a chair on the stage next to Principal Taylor with a few other school officials when I walk inside the auditorium. They're deep in conversation. I know this impromptu gathering is about Chaos. I take the end seat in the first row.

"Hi, good looking," the platinum blond from the other night says.

I don't remember her name. I have to admit she does look good. My old self would've been all over her to hit that. She glares at the girl sitting next to me.

"Move, bitch. You're in my seat."

The girl scrambles out of the chair to find another one. Platinum Blond squeezes past me and makes sure she puts as much of her ass in my face as possible. When she takes the now-available space, she pushes her breasts into my arm. My eyes clash with Cin's when I look forward. I waited around in the living room and kitchen to catch a glimpse of her yesterday like a fucking fool. Only to discover she left early that morning—to stay clear of me, most likely. She makes me forget—only temporarily, but still—she provides me with a high stronger than cocaine. When I bumped into her this morning while jogging, I wanted to drag her into a nearby ditch and fuck her senseless. She can deny it all she wants, but she wanted it just as much as I did. *Want.* The only thing I've *wanted* for the last few years was to die.

"How are you liking Longhorn County so far?" she bats her fake eyelashes.

"I don't."

"Me either. I can't wait to get the fuck out of here. I'm having a party on Saturday, and you're on the VIP list."

"Really? What makes me so special?"

"Do you really have to ask?"

She slides her hand up my thigh. I grab her wrist to stop her from touching my dick.

"Keep your hands to yourself." I flick her hand away.

"We can find somewhere private after the assembly."

I don't bother to provide her with a response.

"Good morning. May I have everyone's attention, please," Principal Taylor announces into a microphone from the podium.

The students continue their loud chatter. Sheriff Andy steps up to speak, guiding Principal Taylor to the side.

"So are you coming?" she asks.

"Sure."

More than likely Cin will be there too, which means I'm definitely going.

"Good. Starts at ten. Maybe you'll get lucky."

"Mouths shut and eyes forward!" the sheriff shouts.

That pronouncement officially silences everyone in the auditorium.

"Thank you, Sheriff Andy." Principal Taylor takes his spot behind the podium again. "A very disturbing report was brought to my attention early this morning, regarding vandalism at McKinley High School over the winter break."

The senior class erupts in cheers.

"Quiet! This is a very serious matter. The perpetrators will be caught and prosecuted to the fullest extent of the law. I implore anyone with information pertaining to this incident to see me immediately."

The principal hands the microphone to the sheriff.

"An investigation is underway, and it will continue until those who are responsible are found."

The sheriff hands the microphone back to the principal.

"Though the new year started off on a negative note, I'm optimistic the school year will end on a positive one. You are dismissed to go to second period, which will begin in a few minutes."

I stand and walk towards the exit, dismissing What's Her Name. Josh pops up at my side.

"Keep your fucking mouth shut," he says.

"And if I don't?" I ask.

"I'll make your life a living hell."

I blow him a kiss. "My life is already a living hell."

Cin

My eyes have constantly drifted to the entrance of the cafeteria for the last fifteen minutes. Art hasn't made an appearance yet. Maybe he decided to skip lunch. So far Art and I only have first period together, but he could still be in one of my afternoon classes. I sit at the table with the crew.

"Don't forget about my party this Saturday. My parents won't be back until Sunday night," Bri says.

"It's time to get high, drunk, and laid!" Danny exclaims.

"Hell yeah, man," Aiden says, high-fiving Danny.

"Josh, where's Art?" Lilah asks.

"Do I look like his fucking keeper? I don't give two shits where he is."

"That fuckwad is in first period with Cin and me. I was about to kick his ass. Tell your cousin to keep his eyes off my girl before I beat the shit out of him."

Josh's eyes roam over my face to search my reaction to Trevor's comment. "He bothering you, Cin? I'll let my dad know so he can get the boot."

"He's not bothering me. He only wanted to bait Trevor, and it worked," I reply.

I can't jump on the "let's crucify Art" bandwagon. He's hurting. His cries break my heart.

"As if he wants Cin," Bri scoffs. "He can't stop looking at me."

Lilah rolls her eyes. "That's where you're mistaken. He wants me."

"Fuck him. You both can have me. You know what? I have a great idea. How about we have a threesome on Saturday?" Danny waggles his eyebrows, throwing his arm around Bri's shoulders.

She shrugs him off. "Oh, you already had your chance, so I'll pass."

"Fuck you then."

Robbie looks at Bri. "Did you invite him to your party?"

"Duh. Why wouldn't I?"

"Fuck, come on, Bri," Robbie says grouchily.

"Hey, it's my party, and I'll invite whoever I want. If you don't like it, stay home."

"If he steps out of line, we'll fuck him up." Zeke cracks his knuckles.

"Do you want your nose broken again?" Dex muses.

"I swear to God, Dex, you say one more thing about my nose, it's going to be curtains for your ass."

"There'll be absolutely no fighting in my house. I mean it. If my parents find out I had a party, I'm toast. I'll be punished for the rest of the school year."

"He was just defending himself since you're all a bunch of bullies," Anneli remarks.

The boys grumble but make no comment.

"He tried to kill himself," Josh says.

I jerk my head in his direction, and so does everyone else.

"Josh," I admonish.

"What? It's true."

"You're shitting me," Danny says in disbelief.

"I shit you not. After his brother died, Art went…" He circles his index finger at his temple.

"How did he do it?" Aiden asks.

"He slit his wrists. That's why he wears the leather wristbands—to hide the scars. My father found him."

"How did his brother die?" Bri asks.

"He drowned in the swimming pool. Art found him."

"That's awful," Anneli says.

"He's been fucked up ever since," Josh says.

"Still want to fuck him, Bri? You'll end up like that blond chick in that Norman Bates movie," Zeke says.

"That makes him more appealing. The tortured souls fuck the best," Bri replies.

"Speak of the devil," Aiden says, jutting his chin towards the entrance.

ART

I automatically seek her out the moment I walk through the cafeteria door. There she is at the "popular kids" table, with everyone from Chaos night. I walk over to the serving station to examine the fare this school has to offer. I wouldn't feed this bullshit to a dog. I'd rather eat Missy's chicken Marsala. I opt to grab a bottled water before heading to an empty table. A shadow falls over me while I'm scrolling through my cell phone. The kid standing beside the table looks like he stepped right out of an eighties' rock music video—heavy eyeliner, long messy hair, nail polish, platform shoes, everything black from head to toe. His face is covered in piercings. He pops his gum, wearing a stupid grin on his face.

"Can I help you?" I ask.

"I'm Bane," he says, sitting in the chair next to me.

I take a drink of water. "And I'm 'I don't give a fuck.'"

"You're hilarious."

"What the fuck do you want?"

"Word on the street is you're Josh's cousin."

"If you have a point, get to it." I'm losing my patience fast.

"Why are you sitting here alone?" He pops his gum. "And not over there with the rulers of Central High School?"

"I don't need a clique to feel like I belong."

"You can sit with me and my friends."

"I'm not looking to make friends," I say.

Hopefully he'll read between the damn lines and get the hell away from me.

"Hey, man, that's cool. If you need anything, let me know. I got the hookup on weed, ecstasy, meth, speed, cocaine… You name it."

I'm on the verge of hyperventilating when the word *cocaine* leaves his mouth. I react the only way I know how, with violence. I punch him in the face, causing him to fall from the chair and hit the floor.

"Get the fuck out of my sight before I fuck you up."

He stumbles to his feet as blood seeps from his mouth. "What the fuck is wrong with you, man?" he asks.

Some are oblivious to what is going on, while others look on with avid interest. Everyone at Josh's table watches as the drama unfolds. When a group of students, whom I assume are his friends, start to approach, I stand and grab a chair.

"Tell your friends to back the fuck off or it's going to get real *WrestleMania*, quick."

He peers behind him and waves his friends off, then turns back around to face me. "We could've been cool, man."

"Come near me again, and I'll break your neck," I threaten before leaving the cafeteria.

I knew it was a fucking bad idea to come in here.

Cin

"Hey, babe," Trevor calls as he approaches me.

"Hey," I greet him, giving him a peck on the lips.

"Are you going to run a few laps around the track after school?" he asks.

"Yeah, with Anneli," I answer, closing my locker.

"Do you want to come over after? We can do our homework together."

"Oh, I know what you want to do, and it isn't homework." I chuckle.

"Can't we do both?" He gives me his signature lopsided smile.

"Depends, will your parents be home?"

His mom is always lurking around, and we were almost caught in the act a few times. She doesn't turn in for the night until I leave. His father doesn't give two shits if his teenage son is sexually active though.

Trevor kisses the side of my neck. "It's date night, so my parents won't be home until late."

"We can do both after all," I reply, closing my locker.

"I bought you more thongs."

"Oh, I bet you did."

Trevor fucks me the hardest when I wear a sexy pair of panties. It's his fetish.

He waggles his eyebrows. "Come on, I'll walk you to class."

Trevor circles his arm around my shoulders as we walk down the hall. I can't stop myself from thinking about Art, as usual. I haven't seen him since he stormed out of the cafeteria. I was on pins and needles walking to class after lunch, wondering if Art would be in class with me, but he never showed. The day isn't over yet though. I still have two more classes. Bane must've said something to piss Art off enough for him to punch him in the face. His enemy list keeps growing by the second. Soon, he'll have the whole school against him.

"Okay, see you later, babe." Trevor hits my butt as I enter the classroom.

I giggle. "Later, babe."

I scan the room. No Art. Class hasn't started yet, so he could still come within the next five minutes. I make my way to the back of the classroom—where I can hide from the teacher and hope never to be called on to answer a question I have no idea how to respond to—and sit next to a boy I've seen around school but whose name I don't recall. My breathing speeds up when Art walks through the door and his eyes land on me. He comes to a stop in front of the boy sitting next to me.

He doesn't say anything, merely stands there until the boy fidgets uncomfortably and gets up to find another desk. Art sits in the now-unoccupied seat next to me. I look over at him.

"If you keep up with that attitude, you'll have the whole senior class gunning for you," I say.

"Do I look afraid?" he asks.

"So, it's you against the whole world?"

"No, it's me against the universe."

"Can't you at least try to fit in?"

"I don't want to fit in."

"What happened between you and Bane?"

"He got on my bad side."

"But isn't everyone on your bad side?"

Before he can answer, the bell rings and the teacher strolls into the classroom. The chatter comes to a halt.

"Welcome to the new year, ladies and gentleman. My name is Mr. Hall. We're going to have a lovely time in trigonometry."

I block out what Mr. Hall is saying.

"Do you jog every morning?" I ask in a low voice.

"No, only when I'm restless. You?"
"Yes, it's good exercise, and I'm on the track team."

"You any good?"
"Yep, I have a full scholarship to Lexington University."
"I've heard of it. It's located in Cali, right?"
"Yes."
"What races do you run?"
"I've been participating in the one-, two-, and four-hundred-meter dash since elementary school."
"I guess that means you and Trevor are going to call it quits after graduation since you're moving thousands of miles away."
"We're not. Trevor applied to Lexington. He's still waiting on a response."
"What if he doesn't get accepted?"
"He's applied to other schools in the area."
"Figures. He seems like the type to follow you around like a fly to horse manure."
"There's nothing wrong with a guy wanting to be near his girlfriend. What are your plans after high school?"
"I don't have any. Did you fuck him yesterday?"
"That's none of your damn business," I snap.

"You left at the crack of dawn and didn't get home until late, all to avoid me. Do I have that much of an effect on you?"

"Get over yourself," I scoff, but I know he can see right through my bullshit.

"Did you think about me when he was fucking you?"

Yes.

I turn my attention to the front of the classroom, planning to ignore him.

He leans over to whisper in my ear. "You can pretend like you don't want to fuck me as much as I want to fuck you if it makes you feel like a better person."

He grasps my knee.

"Come to my bedroom tonight. No one has to know."

No one has to know.

He's the snake in the Garden of Eden, coercing me to take a bite of the forbidden fruit. I grip the edge of the desk with sweaty palms, still looking forward. I clench my thighs together because his words conjure images I shouldn't be thinking of.

"You want to feel my dick inside you. Be honest with yourself."

I love Trevor, I do, but when Art entered the picture, everything became muddled.

"You're clenching your thighs together. Tell me. Is your pussy wet?" He licks my ear.

When the bell rings, I race from the classroom. Why do I want him? My life was so perfect before he came here. I'm tempted—I'm so fucking tempted. I hope he's not in my last class of the day.

"What's the matter?" Anneli asks. She keeps pace with me while we run laps around the track.

"Nothing. Why are you asking?"

"You seem distracted."

"I'm fine."

"You know you can tell me anything. I know when something is bothering you."

"There's just been a lot going on with Art moving in."

"You said he wasn't bothering you."

"He's not."

"Then what's going on?"

"I'm nervous about track season. First practice will be here before we know it. I have to get in shape if I want to beat the competition this year."

"You've never been nervous about track before. Anyway, you're already set, so don't overthink things."

"I still want to get first place this year."

"Don't worry. You will."

I have to get Art out of my thoughts, but it's impossible. Maybe I'll spend the weekend at Lilah's house so I can put some distance between us.

"You know it's going to be trouble at Bri's party Saturday night when Art arrives. With him on the guys' shit list and Bri and Lilah fighting over him, it's going to be a disaster." Anneli rubs her forehead.

I can only imagine.

Chapter Fourteen

Cin

Friday came and went without a hitch. Art played nice with his peers. Except me, that is. He teased me at every opportunity. No matter where I sit in trigonometry class, he follows me. I stood at his bedroom door with my ear pressed against it again last night and listened while he relived the day he found his brother floating in the pool. I wonder if he cut himself. How can pain ease pain? I wanted to go inside to offer comfort, to hold him, but I knew that once I crossed that invisible line, there'd be no going back. He would've taken more from me than comfort, and I would've freely given it to him.

I arrive back at the house after my morning jog, but instead of heading inside, I walk over to the building that houses the sweet potatoes and slips. I bag up a few for breakfast. When I hear the door open, I glance over, expecting Ricky, but instead it's the boy I can't get out of my mind.

His gaze slides over the contents in the room before settling on me. "What are those?" He tilts his head towards the pots covering the tables throughout the large open space.

"This is where the slips are stored in the winter. The temperature in here is kept between fifty and sixty degrees to trigger dormancy. If it's too cold, the slips will freeze, and if it's too hot, they'll dry out and can't be used when planting season starts."

"What are slips?"

"They're vines that grow out of the sweet potatoes. They're planted to grow more sweet potatoes."

"Why is it so dark in here?" Art moves closer to me with each question he asks.

"The slips have to be kept in a dark, dry place."

"What are you about to do?"

"Sweet potatoes grown last season are stored in here too. I came to get a few to cook for breakfast."

Now he stands directly in front of me with barely any space separating us. "How do you know all this stuff?"

"I wanted to learn more, so Ricky taught me all there is to know about farming sweet potatoes. Why did you follow me in here?"

"You know why."

"We can't do this, Art."

He grips my hips to pull me towards him. "Sure we can."

"Trevor—"

"Fuck Trevor."

I drop the bag of sweet potatoes when his lips touch mine. A zing of electricity jolts through my core. His tongue massages the inside of my mouth. I moan into the kiss. We're drowning in each other, our lips perfectly in sync as we share oxygen. When he exhales, I inhale. I glide my hands up his chest before pushing him away.

"Stop." I spin around to run from the building, forgetting all about the sweet potatoes.

"Where the fuck are you going?" he growls.

He takes hold of my long ponytail and clasps the back of my neck, then swings me around to face him. I whimper when he moves his hand from my neck to crush my jaw in a bruising grip. He resumes the kiss with force. I open my mouth to accept his invading tongue, because what the fuck else am I supposed to do?

He releases my hair to slide his hand down my back to clutch my ass. He grinds his hard length into me. I jerk my head to the side to end the kiss, but that doesn't deter him. He kisses down the side of my neck.

"I can't do this." I need to think clearly.

"But you want to. I promise it'll be our little secret."
"No," I groan.

I stop him the only way I know how. I scream, loud and long. He releases me, startled. I use his moment of distraction to tear away from him and make a run for it. The house is still quiet when I burst through the door, so no one heard my scream. That's a good thing. I go to the kitchen to prep for breakfast. I'll go back to get the sweet potatoes in a few minutes, when I'm sure Art will be gone. I wash my hands, then open the refrigerator to take out what I need.

Bacon, eggs, butter...

I glance over my shoulder when I hear the kitchen door open. I place the items on the counter, never taking my eyes from him. I fully face him to prepare for what's next.

He holds up the bag of sweet potatoes. "Where do you want these?"

That's an unexpected question. "Put them in the sink. I have to wash them off."

He empties the bag of sweet potatoes into the sink, then steps back. I walk over cautiously and turn on the faucet to begin washing them off. I'm nervous because my back is to him, but he's not stupid enough to try anything, especially when anyone could walk in at any moment.

I feel the heat of him behind me before he touches me. I should've known not to underestimate him. He slides his hands inside my panties. I grasp the edge of the sink.

"What are you doing? Someone could come in and see us."

His response is to lick and nibble on my neck. I bite my bottom lip to prevent myself from crying out loud when his finger moves over my clit in a frantic motion. My head drops back to loll against his hard chest. His other hand moves lower until a finger enters my opening. I widen my stance while his hands work vigorously between my legs. I can't control the loud moans that leave my mouth, even with the prospect of being caught.

"You're so fucking wet. The next time it'll be my dick penetrating your cunt. It's going to happen. Face it. I'm not trying to break up your happy relationship. I just want a piece of you." He pushes his hard thickness against my ass as he thrusts his finger. I rise to the tip of my toes with each forceful stroke.

I hear the front door open. Fuck, somebody's up.

"Art, you have to stop." I struggle to break free.

"Not until you come."

I feel my orgasm building, gaining momentum as his hands pick up speed. The muscles of my stomach spasm uncontrollably the moment my climax hits. I gasp for air as he moans.

"The way your pussy clenches my finger makes me want to fuck you where you stand." He pulls his hands from my sweatpants mere moments before Ricky walks through the kitchen door. His gaze moves from Art to me. I turn my face away quickly, sure he'll see the guilt written there.

"What's going on here?" he asks.

"Cin gave me a lesson about sweet potato farming. To show my appreciation, I'm helping her wash some for breakfast."

"Oh, that's good. I'm glad you two are getting along now. Cin, you're shaking. Are you okay?"

"Yes, I think I overdid it on my jog," I answer without looking at him.

"Don't push yourself so hard, sweetie."

I nod.

"Well, I'm ready for some coffee," he says, walking over to the coffee maker.

CHAPTER fifteen

 ART

Where the fuck is she?

I got to this fucking party an hour ago, but still no Cin. I thought she would've arrived by now since she was already gone when I left the house. The whole dickhead brigade is here though. Every once in a while, Josh's friends glance over at where I am sitting on the sectional. I swear if those fuckers move in my direction, this place is going to look like a landfill when I'm done beating their asses. From the moment I stepped through the door, Bri—she told me her name again—has been glued to my side. She's practically sitting in my lap. Lilah glares daggers at her. I continuously eye the front door. The house is filled with music, dancing, beer, and weed.

"What do you say?" Bri asks.

"About what?"

"Do you want to go upstairs, silly?" She laughs.

"No," I respond.

"Okay, it's still early. We can go up later."

Does she not know when to take a hint?

"You fucking bitch!" she suddenly yells, running to the landing of the stairs. There's a little girl sitting on the last step. She appears to be around ten years old. She must be Bri's younger sister.

"Go to your fucking room!"

"Why? I'm not doing anything," she whines.

"Get upstairs right now before I kick your skinny ass."

"I'll tell Mom and Dad you had a party when they get home."

"If you do, you'll regret it!" Bri grabs her wrist.

"Ouch!" the girl shouts.

"You open your mouth, and I'll make your life a living hell," Bri warns, pulling her sister upstairs.

I almost come to the girl's aid. Bri should cherish her little sister because life can change drastically in the blink of an eye. I wish Cole were here to get on my fucking nerves. Lilah sits beside me.

"I can suck your dick and make you come in under five minutes."

My dick doesn't even twitch at her proclamation.

Before I can respond to her comment, Cin walks through the front door with her bitch ass boyfriend. Gone are the baggy unflattering clothes she usually sports. She's wearing a tight low-cut black shirt, a mini denim skirt, and thigh-high boots. Her beautiful hair flows around her. Lilah is still talking at my side, but I don't know what the fuck she's saying. The pair walk over to their friends.

"Are you listening to me?" Lilah asks.

"No."

"Fuck you," she replies, leaving the sectional.

Well at least she got the hint, unlike Bri. Cin hasn't glanced my way since she walked through the fucking door. Trevor drags her to the middle of the living room where several couples are dancing. She wraps her arms around his neck. His hands grip the cuff of her ass cheeks. Their bodies meld together as they move to the sensual beat of the music.

She laughs when he whispers something in her ear, then his mouth latches onto hers. I want to be the one to incite her laughter. I feel my anger rising.

Why do I feel this way? She means nothing to me. Fuck, I was living in a world of turmoil before relocating here. Guilt was my sole emotion, but now I'm starting to feel something else entirely. That's not fair to Cole. Thoughts of him should always be in the forefront of my mind. Once I graduate, Cin won't matter anymore. The likelihood of me seeing her again will be slim, and I'll be able to go back to my pathetic existence. I'm going to prove she doesn't mean a damn thing to me. I'm tired of self-induced orgasms anyway. My eyes scan the room until they land on Lilah. She's talking with a group of girls near the kitchen. Hopefully her offer still stands. I walk up to her.

"Let's go upstairs," I say, effectively ending their conversation.

A wide smile spreads across her lips as her eyes light up. "Sure."

I grab her wrist, pulling her past Cin and Trevor and up the stairs. When we reach the top, I spot Bri coming down the hall.

"What the fuck is this?"

She glances from my hand circled around Lilah's wrist to my face.

"Lilah offered to suck my dick and make me come in less than five minutes."

Bri's face scrunches in fury. "Bitch!"

"He's not your boyfriend."

"I can suck your dick better than she can," Bri announces.

"You both can suck my dick," I suggest.

"I'm game. Are you?" Bri arches her eyebrow.

"Absolutely. Lead the way," Lilah answers.

Bri turns on her heel. We follow her down the hall to a door on the right. She pushes it open, and we follow behind her. My eyes roam around the room when she flicks on the light. This must be her bedroom. I release Lilah's wrist to walk over to the bed. I tug my jeans and boxers down to my ankles before sitting.

"Are instructions needed?" I ask when neither of them makes a move.

Lilah sits beside me while Bri kneels between my legs. Lilah strokes my length until it's at full mast.

"You're so big," Lilah says in amazement.

I lie back against the mattress, folding my hands behind my head. I moan when Lilah's mouth begins to move up and down on my dick. Bri rotates between massaging and sucking my balls. I close my eyes, imagining it's Cin who's sucking my dick. Lilah wasn't fucking kidding. She sucks dick like a fucking porn star. How does a high school girl learn how to deep-throat? I hear a low creak and crack my eyes open to peer towards the door that was left slightly ajar. I see Cin's shocked face, but she doesn't leave. Instead, she watches. Her eyes roam over the scene until they meet mine.

"Shit!" I shout, my cum shooting down Lilah's throat.

Damn, she made me come in less than five minutes like she claimed she could.

My lids drift closed as the last tremors of my climax subside. When I open them again, Cin is gone.

Cin

I can't believe what I just witnessed. I went upstairs to use the bathroom since the one downstairs was occupied. I only walked towards Bri's room because I saw the light was on, and I hadn't seen her since I arrived. Nothing could've prepared me for the scene I happened upon. I felt a surge of jealousy. It's an ugly emotion I shouldn't have. I'm in a relationship. What Lilah, Bri, and Art do shouldn't matter to me, but it does.

Trevor isn't in the living room when I get back, so I make my way to the kitchen. The space is crowded with kids. I'm dismayed to find Danny has started a game of red face. It's something he made up last summer, where two opponents slap each other senseless until one person gets knocked out. He always wins. Each person has to put up twenty dollars to participate. Zeke stands behind Danny in the unlikely event he's finally met his match. Robbie stands behind his unfortunate opponent. I wonder how much is on the line. Trevor, Anneli, Dex, Josh, and Aiden stand together, watching the show. I walk over to join them.

"Are you okay?" Trevor asks.

"I'm fine."

Anneli peers over at me. They're too damn perceptive.

Trevor presses. "You sure?"

"Positive."

"You have a distressed look on your face, like someone hit your puppy."

"No, I'm fine." I laugh it off.

He studies my face.

"How much money is on the table?" I ask, to prevent him from further commenting on my abrupt change in mood.

"It's up to a hundred dollars now. Danny has knocked four people out so far," Trevor answers.

I breathe a sigh of relief when he doesn't ask any more questions.

"Let's go, baby!" Danny shouts.

He brings his arm back as far as he can, then swings it forward full force. The sound of Danny's palm hitting the face of that poor soul resembles an explosion.

Collective screams, shouts, and laughter resound throughout the kitchen.

The boy falls back into Robbie's arms. He's out for the count. Robbie drags his limp body out of the kitchen.

"Who's next?" Danny peers around the room.

No one steps forward.

"Come on, you bunch of pussies! Who wants a piece?" He raises his arms like a rock star entertaining his fans.

"Me."

My head whips in the direction of Art's voice. I hadn't noticed he came into the kitchen.

"No, your money is no good here," Danny says.

Art pulls his wallet from his back pocket. He reaches inside and retrieves a hundred-dollar bill.

"Are you sure about that?" He holds up the money for everyone to see.

All noise ceases. Everyone is waiting to see what happens next. Danny is too greedy to pass up this opportunity. "Okay. Bring it on."

"This isn't going to end well," Anneli says.

"No, it isn't." I agree.

"You got this, Danny. Slap the shit out of his ass!" Aiden yells.

Art places the money on the counter, then takes a stance before Danny.

Robbie walks back in. "What the hell? I'm not spotting him."

"I'll spot him," Dex says, stepping behind Art.

Bri and Lilah walk into the kitchen.

"Where were you two?" Anneli asks.

Lilah blushes, while Bri stares at the floor like she sees something interesting.

"You want to go first, bitch?" Danny taunts.

Art smirks. "Ladies first."

A few kids laugh. Danny's hand whips across Art's face without any warning. That was a cheap shot. Art stumbles back a little but recovers superfast, his hand connecting with Danny's face. Danny loses his footing, causing him to bump into Zeke. Blood trickles from the corner of his mouth. He spits in the sink.

There's no cheering. It's deathly silent. Everyone looks on in anticipation, wondering who the victor will be.

They go back and forth, smacking the hell out of each other.

"Josh, this is getting dangerous," I say, a tremor in my voice.

"We broke them up during Chaos. Tonight it ends when one of them falls," Josh replies.

I peer at Trevor, hoping to get him on my side like last time.

"The pissing match between them isn't going to stop, and I'm not getting in the middle of it again. Let them kill each other," Trevor states.

Blood begins to run from Danny's nose. Art's face is showing the effects of the game as well.

Danny appears disoriented, barely able to stand.

Enough is enough.

I move in between them in a quest to end this madness.

"Cin! Get back!" Trevor yells.

But it's too late. Danny's hand hits my face with the force of a supernova, causing my body to spin around. I'm unable to stop myself as I hit the counter, head first.

CHAPTER sixteen

ART

"What the fuck happened?" Ricky is seething with rage. His face is as red as a tomato. That's how pissed he is.

Josh, Trevor, and I don't speak.

"Somebody better start talking now!" he yells.

A few people waiting to receive services in the emergency room watch us where we stand. Cin's mom is with her while she receives a CAT scan. Cin was out cold after her head banged against the counter. Blood poured from a gash just above her left eyebrow. Everyone panicked, including me. Some kids were screaming, others were crying. I was so fucking scared. She seemed so lifeless and her skin started to turn pale. It brought me back to that day. She's hurt, and it's because of me. I didn't help her because I couldn't.

Instead I was in a state of shock. Why am I such a fuck-up? I should have left well enough alone and stayed the fuck away from Danny since he hadn't fucked with me at the party. When I came to my senses, I started beating the fuck out of Danny. It took several people to pull me off him. I'm not sure who called for an ambulance. When the paramedics drove off with her, I hopped on my motorcycle to follow.

"Did you do this, Art?" Ricky asks.

"What the fuck kind of question is that?" I'm about to punch the shit out of my uncle.

"Your face is all fucked up. What am I supposed to think? She could've been defending herself against you," he says.

"I didn't do that to her!" I shout at the top of my lungs.

A security officer starts moving towards us.

"Dad, he didn't do that to Cin," Josh says.

"Then somebody better explain."

"She fell," Trevor answers.

"She fell? Am I supposed to believe that bullshit? Why is there a handprint on her face?"

"Hello, gentlemen. I have to ask you to please keep your voices down," the security officer says.

"Sorry," Ricky says.

"It's what happened," Josh says.

"So that's the story you guys are going to stick to, huh? That still doesn't explain what happened to your face, Art."

No one says a word.

"When she wakes up, she better have the same explanation." Ricky walks off.

"You and Danny messed up big time," Josh says.

"I know," I reply.

I don't know what I'm going to do if her injuries are serious.

"I'm to blame too. Cin wanted me to stop them, but I wouldn't," Trevor says.

"I guess we all share in the blame." Josh rubs the back of his neck.

Sometime later Ricky returns with Cin's mother. Josh and Trevor don't give a fuck about me, but our concern for Cin keeps us together. We stand at their approach.

"How is she?" I ask.

"She's doing well, but she does have a concussion. The gash on her eye looks a lot worse than it really is. The doctor wants her to remain here for a few more hours, just to be on the safe side," Missy answers.

"Is she awake?" Trevor asks.

"She was for a bit, but she fell asleep again. The doctor said she needs to rest, so no visitors. Go home, boys. She'll be coming home in a few hours. Trevor, I'll give you a phone call later."

Cin

Dawn is breaking over the horizon by the time we make it home. My mom helps me upstairs and into bed. My eye is swollen shut, and I have a massive migraine.

She kisses my forehead. "Send me a text if you need anything."

I keep my eyes closed because the world spins around me when I open them. Any movement of my head causes severe pain, so I give her the "okay" hand gesture instead of nodding. I hear the click of my door closing, but after a few minutes, I hear it open again. I crack my eyes open.

"That was really stupid of you." Art moves towards the bed.

"Have you heard of knocking?"

"Why on earth would you jump in the middle of us? You're lucky all you got was a concussion."

"What you and Danny were doing was stupid and dangerous. What would've happened if I hadn't intervened?"

"That's not your concern. You put yourself at risk. Next time, stay out of it."

"If there's a next time, I'll jump in the middle of it again."

"Goddamn it, Cin."

I whimper.

"What is it?"

"My head hurts so bad."

"Didn't the doctors give you medicine?"

"Yes, and a prescription, but it only lessens the pain."

"I'll get you some ice to put on your eye."

"Thank you."

A few minutes later, Art returns. He lies on the bed beside me, guiding my head onto his chest to hold the bag of ice on my eye. He runs his fingers through my hair. I relax against him, enjoying the scalp massage he's giving me.

"I saw you watching us."

"I was not watching," I sputter.

"You were."

"I wasn't. So are you all in a poly-relationship now?" I ask.

He laughs. "Not hardly."

"You seemed to be enjoying yourself quite a bit."

"So, you admit you were watching."

"I just glanced."

"If you say so."

"What the fuck is this?" Trevor snarls.

"Art got some ice for me because my eye is killing me."

"I can take over from here."

The instant tension in my bedroom is suffocating.

"Art, please go. We already had enough excitement for one night." I'm so exhausted. I can't deal with this right now.

Art gently lowers my head onto the pillow, then guides my hand to the bag of ice before leaving. Trevor takes the space Art vacated seconds ago.

"That was really stupid, Cin."

"So I've been told," I deadpan.

"This is serious!"

I wince. "Lower your voice."

"I'm sorry. I was stupid for not breaking it up when you asked me to."

"I know."

"Rub it in, why don't you?" he jokes, then his tone turns serious. "I don't like that he was holding you."

"He wasn't holding me. He was helping me."

"He was playing with your hair."

"I'm really tired, and I don't feel like fighting."

"Okay, I'll stay here until you fall asleep."

I yawn. "Thank you."

CHAPTER seventeen

Cin

The last week has been boring. I stayed home from school Monday and Tuesday since I still wasn't feeling one hundred percent. Ricky and my mom grilled me about what happened that night, but I told them I couldn't remember. I didn't want to contradict any story that was already told to them. Everyone coddled me and made sure I was comfortable. Art came to my bedroom whenever Trevor wasn't around to stay with me for a while. We barely talked, just idle chitchat here and there, but the silence was nice. Maybe I should smash my face into kitchen counters more often. Though I was given a clean bill of health to go back to school on Wednesday, the doctor told me to take it easy and avoid jogging for the rest of the week. It was really hard not to do something I love. I can't remember a time when jogging wasn't a part of my daily routine.

The bruise on my eye is healing perfectly, but it's still a bit discolored. A light scar will be left for sure. Danny did some epic groveling. It was hilarious. He carried my books, brought lunch to the table for me, and asked if I was okay every five seconds when I was in his presence. It's Saturday again, and I'm determined to go on a morning jog. I rise with the sun, putting on my jogging gear before going downstairs. I walk towards the kitchen to get a drink of water before heading out. Art steps out of the bathroom.

"Good morning," I say.

He doesn't return the greeting. There are heavy bags under his eyes. His nightmares must've kept him up all night.

"Are you okay?"

He walks by me without saying a word.

I grab his arm. "Talk to me."

He slams me against the wall, sliding his forearm across my neck. "We are not friends. Got it?"

I thought he and I had an understanding. His behavior is volatile, like a dog that turns on its owner unexpectedly and without provocation. The demons riding him are relentless in their pursuit to destroy him.

"Stay out of my damn way before I fucking hurt you," he growls.

I drop to my knees when he releases me, gasping for oxygen. He slams his bedroom door shut. How can things change between us within the span of a few days? I clamber to my feet and storm towards his bedroom to demand he tell me what the fuck his problem is. My courage evaporates the moment my hand grasps the doorknob. I know if I enter his bedroom, something will happen that can't be undone. I don't know if that's something I'm willing to risk. Art is a wild card. I turn away a little less excited about my morning jog.

ART

I stand at the door willing her to come in. My body vibrates with energy. My control is hanging by a thread.

Open the door. Open the door. Open the door... I continuously chant inside my head. I swear to fucking God, if she opens that door I'll be balls deep in her cunt with her face buried in the mattress in less than five seconds. When she releases the door and leaves, I almost go after her to drag her in here whether she wants to come or not. Instead, I punch holes in the wall until my fists bleed.

Thoughts of Cole haunt my dreams until I wake up in a cold sweat, but the end of the dream isn't the end of my torment. My brain will not shut down—it is on replay, that night running through my head over and over again. I reach for my razor and begin cutting myself, to get my mind off Cole, and it helps for a little while. I don't know how much longer I can live like this.

I open my eyes to the sound of someone knocking on my door. I'm not good company to be around today, so for the most part I've stayed in my bedroom.

"Open up. It's your favorite cousin."

I'm definitely not responding to that motherfucker, but the bastard comes in, uninvited. Fuck, I should've locked the damn door.

"It's time to get up, asshole," Josh says.

I move into a sitting position to face him. "Get the hell out."

"Daddy Dearest is worried about you, so you're going to participate in Chaos tonight."

"No, I'm not."

"Dude, what the fuck did you do to the wall?" He walks over to inspect the damage.

"The same thing I'm going to do to your face if you don't get out of here."

"Now, what did the wall ever do to you? You are all kinds of crazy, aren't you?" He shakes his head.

"Five, four, three…" I count down as I leave the bed. He's going to look like the wall when I'm through with him.

"Asshole, my father keeps giving me shit about not making you feel welcomed and not inviting you out. I want him off my case."

"Sounds like a personal problem," I retort.

"If you don't come, I'll tell him about your little art project over here." He points at the damaged plaster. "Do you honestly want to spend your Saturday night talking about your feelings with my father?"

I stop in my tracks, snarling like a wild animal.

Josh smirks, folding his arms across his chest. "Let's go. We leave now. It's only the guys tonight."

Just what I fucking need.

Five minutes later, I grudgingly walk with Josh to his truck. It's a little after ten.

"You and Danny play nice tonight, okay?"

"I'm not making any promises."

"Figures," he grumbles, getting into his truck.

"What are we doing tonight? Raiding the Depends stash at a nursing home?"

"Very funny." He gives me the finger.

"Well, you know me, always the jokester."

"You're not opposed to grand theft auto, are you?"

"What type of shit are you assholes going to get into tonight?"

"Just a little joyriding." Josh winks.

"Whatever."

Josh parks in front of a medium-sized house about thirty minutes later.

"Where are we?" I peer around the residential neighborhood.

"Zeke's house."

"I'm not going in there."

I know blood is going to spill if I go in that motherfucker's house.

"I'm not either. Our ride is almost here."

Zeke, Trevor, and Dex emerge from the house when an old white van parks behind Josh's truck.

"We're joyriding in that piece of shit?"

Josh laughs. "Not in the least. That piece of shit is going to get us to our destination."

He pulls a pair of latex gloves from his pocket and holds them out to me.

"The van is stolen. If you don't want your fingerprints left at the scene of the crime, I suggest you wear them," he says.

I take the offered gloves before exiting the truck.

I force my hands into the small pair of gloves. "My hands can barely fit in these tiny fucking gloves."

"Medium was the only size left at the store." Josh shrugs his shoulders.

"Where are Aiden and Robbie?" Josh gives his boys dap.

"They had to deal with some family shit," Trevor answers.

Vineyard Baptist Church is displayed on the side of the van.

"Nice touch, stealing a van from a church." I laugh.

"I thought so," Josh replies.

Danny jumps out of the van, then comes barreling towards me. "Why the fuck is he here, Josh?"

My hands form fists, ready to break this fucker's face if he gets in my personal space.

"Here we go." Dex sighs.

"Stop this shit. The last time got way out of control, and Cin got hurt really bad," Zeke says.

"Well, Cin isn't here now." Danny steps forward.

Josh places his hand on Danny's chest, stopping him. "Zeke's right. You need to calm down. A fight could draw unwanted attention to us. That's something we don't need with a stolen van in our possession."

"Just keep him the hell away from me." Danny storms back into the van.

Josh passes out gloves to the rest of the group.

"It's show time." Dex slides open the van door and climbs in.

Josh gets in the front passenger seat while the rest of us file into the back. I sit in the second row.

Zeke tosses something in my lap. "What's this?"

"It's your disguise, Mr. President." Dex looks back, with a cheeky grin.

I pick up the unknown item to inspect it. It's a Bill Clinton mask. "You've got to be kidding me."

"You'll wear it if you don't want to be identifiable in a police lineup." Dex looks back, sporting a George W. Bush mask.

"We don't need you ratting us out if you get caught," Danny says.

"I'm not a rat. You guys act as if joyriding in a stolen car is a federal offense," I retort.

"It's who the car belongs to that would get us into a heap of trouble if we're caught," Josh says.

"And just whose car will we be joyriding in?" I'm tired of the dramatics.

Danny turns into the parking lot of Judy's, where I had the immense pleasure of kicking his ass for the first time. He comes to a stop beside a blue Subaru.

"Deputy These Nuts. He's a cocky motherfucker who's always on our fucking backs, so it's time to teach him a lesson," Josh answers.

"So we're going to steal a cop's truck?"

"Stealing is such a harsh word. I prefer the term borrowing," Trevor says.

Maybe these guys aren't such pussies after all. It takes brass balls to do the reckless shit they have planned.

"We've been watching him for a while. He comes here every Saturday to eat dinner and flirt with the waitress. He has a major hard-on for her." Josh grins.

"It's time for Chaos!" Dex shouts.

We stealthily leave the van, closing the doors quietly.

Josh is Richard Nixon, Trevor is Ronald Reagan, Zeke is John F. Kennedy, and Danny is Jimmy Carter. We ease into the unlocked Subaru, cat-burglar-like, to avoid detection. Zeke is the driver for tonight's episode of Chaos. Josh sits in the passenger seat beside him. Danny and I sit at opposite ends in the back seat, which is a good thing because I don't want to be hit with an attempted murder charge for throwing the fucker out of a moving vehicle. With the four of us it's a tight fit.

Zeke hotwires the Subaru, then zooms out of the parking lot.

"Woohoo!" Josh shouts with his head hanging out of the window.

The deputy runs out of the diner and chases after his stolen ride. "You fucking kids! I'm going to kick your asses!"

"There you are, Deputy These Nuts. We were looking for you. Thanks for letting us borrow your ride!" Danny yells.

Zeke is doing at least ninety miles per hour. This reckless shit is right up my alley. I'm prepared to die, but I guarantee they're not.

"You guys do know that every cop in the area will be on us in about ten minutes or less," I say.

"Relax, we won't get caught." Dex grins.

Josh switches on the radio and turns the volume up full blast. The tires screech as Zeke jerks the steering wheel right to peel around a corner.

Two police cruisers come out of nowhere behind us, sirens echoing through the night.

"Fuck." Zeke puts the pedal to the metal.

He turns onto a street lined with houses on either side.

"Push it, Zeke! If we get caught, I'm fucked. My dad is going to be beating my ass from now until I graduate college!" Danny yells behind him.

"I'm trying to get us out of this in one piece," he replies.

"Shit, we're going to die," Dex says.

Zeke loses control and crashes into a fire hydrant. Water shoots into the air. The doors swing open and we bolt. The police give chase. I have no idea which way Danny, Dex, Trevor, or Zeke went, but Josh and I end up running in the same direction. I jump over a metal fence surrounding a house and hit the ground running. Josh follows. When I hear a thud, I glance back. Josh is hanging upside down, his foot caught on the fence. I should leave the bitch, but I go back to help him. I jump back over the fence and attempt to free him. His shoe lace is tangled in the metal. The damn gloves make it difficult for me to loosen the laces. *Shit.*

"Shit, they're coming," Josh warns.

I pull the gloves off.

"Hurry up."

"I'm trying, asshole," I snap.

The sounds of the cops' footsteps are getting closer. When I release his foot, he takes off running. I lift my leg, prepared to hop over the fence, but I'm grabbed by my arm and thrown to the ground.

Damn.

Policemen converge on me and a knee rams into the center of my back. My wrists are twisted behind me and handcuffed.

When Art Rises: Living in Cin

Ricky is going to be pissed.

CHAPTER eighteen

Cin

Josh storms past my open door. Something is wrong. Ricky left the house in a fit of anger fifteen minutes earlier. I place the book I'd been reading on the bed before going into Josh's bedroom. I find him pacing, sweating bullets. He's in panic mode and hasn't noticed me.

"What happened?"

He looks over at me, startled. "It's all fucked up, Cin. It's fucked."

I sit on his bed, alarmed.

"We stole Deputy Wyatt's car to joyride in." He sits beside me.

"What the fuck, Josh? Someone could've gotten hurt."

Out of all the idiotic shit I imagined they'd be doing, this possibility never crossed my mind. That's why the guys were quiet about what their plans were for tonight.

"I know. Shit, it wasn't supposed to go down like this. Zeke lost control and crashed." He drags his hand roughly through his hair.

"Is everyone okay? Where's Trevor?" I feel horrible for wanting to ask about Art first.

"Trevor is fine. He doesn't want to face your wrath right now. That's why he hasn't called yet."

"What about everyone else?" I really want to ask if Art is home.

Josh scrubs a hand down his face. "Everyone got away, except Art."

I automatically assume the worst. "Did you guys set him up?"

"How could you even think that? I don't like him, but I wouldn't set him up. It all happened so fast. After Zeke crashed, all of us took off running. Art and I ran in the same direction. I jumped over the fence behind him, but my shoe got stuck. I thought he was going to leave me, but he came back." Josh shakes his head in disbelief. "He got me free, but it was too late for him."

"That's why your father left here furious."

"Fuck, he's going to rat us out." Josh drops his head into his upturned hands.

"Art doesn't seem like the type to snitch, but are you going to let him take the fall by himself?"

"There's no evidence we were involved. We wore masks, so no one can identify our faces. And gloves, so no fingerprints. It'll be our word against his. No one will believe him over us," Josh says with confidence.

Un-fucking-believable.

"How can you throw him to the wolves after he went back for you?" I glower at him.

At least he has the decency to look ashamed. I don't understand why I always feel the need to defend Art, especially since he's such an asshole to me.

"I know you'll do the right thing," I say, leaving his room.

ART

The bastard left me to take all the blame. I can't say I'm surprised. Josh and his friends are snakes. I should've stayed in like I fucking planned, but no, I let the asshole talk me into going out. So here I am at the police station in some shitty interrogation room, getting grilled.

Deputy These Nuts throws the Bill Clinton mask on the table in front of me before leaning close to my face. God, his breath smells like diarrhea.

"Who else was with you tonight? You'll start talking now if you know what's good for you, boy!"

Spittle hits my bottom lip. Fucking disgusting. Sheriff Andy lounges lazily against the wall, his arms crossed over his chest.

"Am I supposed to be scared?"

"You're going to be in juvie until you're twenty! You're a menace to society!" The deputy is getting himself all worked up.

"Let me guess. Good cop." I lift my handcuffed wrists, pointing at Sheriff Andy. "Bad cop." I turn my finger towards Deputy These Nuts.

"What you and your friends did is very serious." Sheriff Andy straightens from the wall.

"I'm ready to talk."

"Good," the deputy says happily.

"I would be doing the entire community a disservice if I didn't tell you how bad your breath stinks. I think it's time you made an appointment to see a dentist. You may have halitosis."

I can almost see the steam coming from his ears. "Someone needs to wring this punk's neck."

"Why don't you do it, Deputy These Nuts?" I challenge.

He wants to beat the fuck out of me. If the sheriff weren't here, he would make a move then come up with some bullshit excuse to explain how I got the bruises. He's the type of motherfucker that was picked on throughout school and became a cop to compensate for his shortcomings. This fucker doesn't need to wield any kind of power. He misuses it.

A light knock sounds at the door. "Come in," the sheriff calls.

Deputy Megan cracks the door open. "Ricky's here, Sheriff." I met her while being escorted through this hellhole.

"Maybe he can talk some sense into you. Let him in." Not likely.

Ricky pushes through the door hard enough for it to bang against the wall.

"Have you lost your fucking mind, Art?" Ricky yells.

"Yeah, about three years ago when I tried to off myself."

"Ricky, we have a real problem here. There were other kids involved, but he won't give them up," Sheriff Andy says.

Ricky rubs his fingers against his temples. "Art—"

"Go ahead and waste your breath. I'm not saying anything."

Ricky slumps his shoulders, defeated. "I know Art well enough to know he isn't going to talk."

"All right, we'll have to lock him up," Sheriff Andy replies.

"Wait a minute. Can I have a private word with you both?" Ricky asks.

There's a tense pause. "Okay, follow me," the sheriff says.

All three leave the room.

Ricky and the sheriff come back into the room about twenty minutes later.

"About fucking time. I have to take a shit," I say.

Sheriff Andy walks over and surprises me by taking off the handcuffs. "You're free to go."

"What?" I rub my sore wrists.

Then it hits me. "How much did the old man pay you to make this disappear? You're nothing but a dirty cop who can be bought. I see where your son gets his morals from." I smirk.

"Watch your mouth, you fucking delinquent." He grasps the front of my shirt.

"Whoa, calm down, Sheriff." Ricky clutches his arm.

"You want to hit me, don't you? Come on. Give me your best shot."

His body trembles with rage. Yeah, he wants to clean my clock.

"Art, shut your damn mouth," Ricky hisses.

He lets my shirt go. "Keep your head down. Your grandfather won't be able to help you next time."

"Sure he will. All he has to do is add more zeros to the check."

"Get him the hell out of here before I do something that'll cause me to lose my job."

I leave the room, not waiting for Ricky. The sheriff can kiss my ass. I brush by Deputy These Nuts on the way out of the building. He doesn't have to open his mouth. The expression on his face tells me everything I need to know—he'll be gunning for me now.

Ricky catches up to me in the parking lot. "What you did tonight was reckless."

"Well, you know reckless is my middle name." I yank the door to Ricky's truck open, then get in.

He starts the ignition. "Were Josh and his friends involved?"

"You'll have to ask Josh that question. How much did the old man pay him?"

"It doesn't matter. He wants you to go live with him since I'm not capable of handling you—his words. Shit, maybe he's right."

"Like he'd do any better. Anyway, I won't go."

"If you keep screwing up, I'll have no choice but to ship you to him."

"The day he comes for me will be the day I disappear."

He controlled my father. I'll be damned if I allow him to control me.

CHAPTER nineteen

Cin

I lie on my stomach across the bed, glowering down at Trevor's digital image through video chat.

"Babe, I'm sorry."

He gives me his best sad puppy-face expression. I cock an eyebrow to let him know that look is not going to get him out of the doghouse.

"What you guys did was really shitty." I roll onto my back, holding my cell phone above me.

"Come on, Cin, give me a break."

"So many things could've gone wrong. Chaos is getting way out of control."

"Well, during Chaos, if you're not out of control—"

"Don't you dare finish that sentence."

"Look on the bright side. Maybe Ricky will get rid of Art now."

I should want him gone, but I don't. "That's what you want, right?"

Damn, I need to learn how to control my facial expressions. "Yeah."

I hear the rumble of an engine outside.

"They're here." I walk over to the window. "I have to go."

"Call me later to let me know what happens."

"Okay." I end the video chat.

I watch as Ricky and Art exit the truck and walk up the porch steps. It's nearly one o'clock in the morning, but I couldn't go to sleep until Art got home.

"Josh, get down here," Ricky yells.

"Do the right thing," I tell Josh as he walks by my door.

ART

I watch Josh descend the stairs, wanting to knock his teeth down his throat. He won't even look at me—straight bitch.

"Talk," Ricky demands when he clears the last step.

"Talk about what?" Josh rubs his chin, acting dumbfounded and shit. Here comes the "I don't know what you're talking about" act.

"You know what, Josh? I have zero fucking tolerance for your bullshit right now."

"I don't know what you're talking about." Josh's face reflects confusion. Somebody should give this bastard an academy award—he's a hell of an actor.

"Art didn't steal Deputy Wyatt's truck on his own. This has you and your friends' names written all over it."

"His truck was stolen?"

Ricky turns to me. "Now is the time to speak up."

He lets out a frustrated growl when I don't provide the information he seeks.

"Listen, Josh, I wasn't born yesterday. If I find out you had anything to do with what happened today, your ass is grass." Ricky disappears upstairs.

Josh finally looks at me. I walk up to him until we're standing toe to toe. "I proved I'm not a rat, but we know who the snakes are."

His nostrils flare. "There's no point in us all going down."

"You're nothing but a dishonest piece of shit."

"You better step back, out of my face."

"Make me." I notice his hands twitching. "Go ahead. Take your best shot."

"Stop. No fighting," Cin says in a low voice as she races down the stairs.

She tries unsuccessfully to separate us.

"Josh, please just come upstairs." She attempts to pull him away. "If you two fight, I'm going to jump smack in the middle, and I could get hurt."

He turns around, following behind Cin.

"She saved you, little bitch."

He stops in his tracks and stiffens.

"Don't let him get under your skin."

Anger morphs into lust as my eyes follow Cin. The tiny pink shorts she's wearing barely cover her ass and the cami top molds to her breasts perfectly. My dick hardens as need consumes me. Fuck—I want her. I want her bad. Once she's out of sight, I storm into my bedroom and close the door. I sit on the bed, pulling out my erection, intent on finding release. My hand rapidly moves up and down my length while I imagine pounding between Cin's legs, but the orgasm I desperately crave eludes me.

Shit! I can't come. Jerking off isn't going to work for the massive hard-on I have. I need to be buried in her heat. Giving up, I put my dick back inside my jeans and circle the room in agitation, leaving footprints in the worn carpet. Thoughts of Cole and cocaine have been in the forefront of my mind for so long, but now Cin is beginning to take center stage. Damn it, I can't allow that to happen. Spending my remaining days on earth experiencing pleasure, when Cole will never feel that emotion again, is not an option. I open the dresser drawer, retrieving the razor stored there, needing an escape. I slash my abdomen in long, deep strokes, deeper than I've ever cut myself. But I'm careful, so stitches aren't needed. Blood drips down my stomach. *Blissful relief.* Unfortunately it only lasts seconds, so I keep going. By the time I'm satisfied the front of my jeans are soaked in blood. I take them off and hold the ruined denim against my abdomen to stop the flow of blood. I lie on the bed, hoping the pain will keep me from finding slumber. Sleep isn't kind to me.

"Please, no. Cole, come back. I'm sorry... so sorry. It should've been me. Why wasn't I there?" My sweaty limbs become entangled in the bedding as I toss and turn. I unsuccessfully will myself to wake up.

"Art. It's okay. You're just having a nightmare."

Though the sound of Cin's voice is music to my ears, it's muffled, as if I'm underwater. When I feel the light touch of fingertips wiping my tears away, my eyes pop open. It's like her touch turned on a switch inside me.

"I warned you," I growl.

I maneuver Cin under me in an instant, pinning her wrists to the bed above her head. My hips settle between her soft thighs—my dick growing harder by the second. I'm going to murder her fucking pussy. Her eyes widen in fear, but I don't give a shit. She whimpers when I bite down on her earlobe.

"You don't fucking listen. Now I'm going to give us what we've been denying each other for far too long."

I capture her lips in a feral kiss. My free hand disappears into her pink shorts, sliding through her slick cunt.

"My God, your wet pussy tells me everything I need to know. I won't be gentle with you. I can't," I whisper against her lips.

Her hips jerk convulsively as my finger circles her clit.

"Careful, it seems as if you like this a bit too much. You're not going to beg me to stop this time? Where are your tears? I was hoping for more."

"I can't fight you anymore," she says, kissing my lips softly.

Her compliance is unexpected but welcomed.

"I want you." She places kisses along my face before wrapping her legs around my back, bringing her sweet heat closer to my throbbing erection.

What little control I had left vanishes. I tear at her clothes like a madman until she's naked, her shirt and shorts in tatters on the floor. I don't fuck her right away. Instead, I kneel between her spread legs. *Fucking gorgeous.* I lift her legs over my shoulders and position my length at her entrance. I thrust forward, not allowing her body time to adjust to my intrusion. She lets out a pained scream as I savagely rip through her tight channel until my dick is completely enveloped by her hot pussy. An animalistic sound escapes my throat. Being inside her is pure ecstasy. I brutally propel my hips forward, trying to imprint her body into the fucking mattress.

"Ugh," she groans, placing her hands on my chest to slow my assault on her dripping pussy. "Be gentle."

"Even if I wanted to I couldn't. I don't have the ability to control myself with you."

I continue punishing her pussy with deep powerful strokes. The bed creaks under the pressure and the headboard bangs against the wall. If anyone happens to venture to the kitchen, the sounds will draw them to my bedroom. The cuts across my stomach begin to bleed, but I'm oblivious to the pain. Her cries of pleasure mixed with grunts of agony echo in my ears.

"Wait, Art, stop. Please," she begs.

Her pleas fall on death ears. A bomb going off couldn't stop me. Her legs tremble as I pound into her like a jackhammer. Damn, her amazing pussy hugs my dick like a fitted glove. Perspiration covers our bodies. With each thrust, her pussy gets wetter and wetter. Goddamn, I'm drowning in it, losing myself in her.

"Fuck," I growl.

I lay flush against her, moving my hips in slow circular motions, savoring the suction of her center on my erection. My hands twist in her hair while I kiss her mouth vigorously, swallowing her moans of bliss. I don't ever remember feeling like this. Her fingernails bite into my back as her heels dig into my ass.

"Art!" she shouts as her orgasm surges through her.

Cin's fluttering cunt milks my manhood, sending me over the edge with her.

"Shit, shit, shit," I chant, emptying my cum inside her.

I give one more thrust, wringing the last of my climax from my body. I lay my head on her shoulder, my semi-hard dick still buried in her warmth. Her thumb brushes across the scar on my wrist.

"You cut yourself really bad this time. You have to stop."

"I need to cut just as much as I need to breathe. It's either cutting or cocaine. Which do you think is better for me?"

There's a long pause.

"Do you dream about your brother every night?"

"Every fucking night since the day he died."

"He's at peace with God."

I raise my head to peer into her eyes. "If there's a God I didn't see him. There isn't a bright light to transport you to paradise when you die. That story is a lie. When I was at death's door, all I saw was a never-ending darkness before I woke up in hell."

She caresses the side of my face. "The only hell you're in is the one inside your mind."

If only that were true, but at least Cin can transport me to paradise for a little while. She gasps when my dick hardens again. We fuck for a few more hours, then she sneaks back up to her bedroom right before dawn.

Chapter Twenty

Cin

What have I done? I ask myself for the millionth time as the water cascades down my body. This is the second time I've betrayed Trevor. After leaving Art's bedroom, I raced upstairs as fast as my feet would carry me, clenching my destroyed clothes to my breasts. There's no way I could explain my naked state if I was seen. I threw my tattered cami and shorts under the bed before wrapping myself in a robe and heading to the bathroom for a shower. If Trevor ever finds out, he'll be heartbroken. What if Art tells him? I can't let this happen again.

I would be lying to myself if I said I didn't enjoy every last minute of Art being inside me. It was passionate and wild, something I've never encountered before. Sex with Trevor is good, but with Art, it's phenomenal. Even though at times it fucking hurt—he was so damn rough—I still wanted more. My hand slides between my legs, gripping my swollen pussy. I groan, circling my clit while flashbacks of Art fucking me filter through my mind. I can't be in the same house with him today. I hurriedly rinse off. I'll spend the day with Anneli because there's no way I can face Trevor, not after what I did.

Hopefully everyone will stay asleep until I'm gone. I dress in a T-shirt and sweatpants. I stuff my ChapStick, car keys, wallet, and cell phone into my pockets before leaving my bedroom. I tiptoe down the stairs, quiet as a mouse. I grasp the doorknob, only moments away from making good on my escape.

"Running away, are we? I knew you would. Can't face what you did in the light of day, can you?"

My body goes rigid, but I don't look back. I pull the door open, prepared to bolt, but Art has other plans. I should've known he wouldn't make this easy for me. He's at my back, pushing the door shut. His large, strong body surrounds my smaller frame. He swings my long braid over my shoulder, skimming soft kisses across the back of my neck. The cool metal of his lip ring slides along my heated flesh. The scent of him calls to my senses, the woodsy aroma making my pussy damp.

"Art, please…"

"Art, please what?"

"I have to go."

"Go where?"

"I have plans."

"Liar."

"What happened was a mistake."

"A mistake you'll make again."

"No."

"Another lie."

I whimper when his hard dick prods my back.

"Go run away, little birdie. I'll be waiting for you when you get back."

Art steps away, taking his warmth with him, leaving me cold.

"Art?"

"Yeah?"

"Will you tell Trevor?"

"The idea of telling him I know how his girl's wet pussy feels is appealing."

"You said it would be our little secret."

"I'll keep my mouth shut. You just be sure to keep your legs open."

I leave the house, walking towards my Toyota Corolla on shaky legs. My cell phone chimes as I slide into the driver's seat.

Trevor: You never called me back. What happened?

Me: I'm sorry. I fell asleep.
Trevor: Are you coming over today?
Me: Not today. Anneli and I are having girl time.
Trevor: I was really hoping to spend some time with you.
Me: I promised Anneli.
Trevor: Okay, come over after school tomorrow.
Me: Okay.

I rest my head against the steering wheel. Shit... I opened Pandora's Box.

"So what's up?" Anneli devours a spoonful of Blue Bell banana pudding ice cream.

When I arrived, she grabbed our favorite treat from the freezer—not the healthiest breakfast but delicious nonetheless. For the last half hour, we've been lounging on her bed talking about the upcoming track and field season.

"What do you mean?"

"Why are you over at my house at seven-thirty in the morning?"

"I didn't know it was a crime to visit a friend," I snap, throwing the spoon in the carton.

"Come on, Cin. You know I didn't mean it like that."

The waterworks start then. God, I'm a complete and utter mess. Anneli leans over, wrapping me in her embrace.

"Oh, sweetie. What happened?"

"I did something really shitty, but that's not the worst part. I liked it, and I want to do it again. I'm afraid of myself."

Though Lilah is my cousin, I have more of a connection with Anneli, and she's not a gossip, so I'm more comfortable talking to her. Anneli is also brutally honest and won't blow smoke up my ass.

"It's not the end of the world," she assures me.

"It feels like it."

"Stop feeling sorry for yourself. What's done can't be undone. The question you have to ask yourself is—what are you going to do to make sure it doesn't happen again? Once is a mistake, twice is inexcusable."

I was so sure of what I wanted before Art came along. Trevor and I have had several long conversations about the future. I know the likelihood of high school sweethearts ending up happily married after college is slim, but Trevor and I were optimistic. I love Trevor. I know my actions say otherwise, but I really do. My feelings for Art are strong, but we could never be together. He's waging a battle inside his mind I can't begin to help him with. Still, I went to his bedroom knowing what would happen.

Once I was sure everyone was asleep, I crept downstairs. I told myself I only wanted to see if he was okay, but we ended up fucking over and over again. The blood seeping from his fresh cuts didn't stop the vigorous thrusts he delivered to my body. Using protection with Art never entered my mind. I know I won't get pregnant since I opted for birth control when I became sexually active with Trevor. Though, to his dismay, I still insisted he wear a condom for a long time afterwards, explaining I wasn't ready for that type of intimacy. Having someone come inside me is a huge deal to me, so I don't understand my decision to let Art break that barrier.

"I'm so ashamed," I whisper as the memory washes over me. Anneli rubs my back.

I cry more. What's going to happen when I go home tonight? Will Art be waiting up for me?

"I know what will make you feel better."

"What?"

"Shopping," she answers with a big smile.

"Shopping makes you feel better." I laugh. Anneli is a certifiable shopaholic. For me, shopping is kryptonite.

"True. Still, I think it'll help take your mind off things."

"All right. I'm in."

"Open your legs, so I can eat your pussy," Art says, kneeling on the bed in front of me.

"We can't," I whisper.

"I'm not leaving until I get a taste." He pulls my panties down my legs.

"This is wrong, so wrong."

"I was never good at doing the right thing."

Art flicks his tongue rapidly across my clit. My back arches off the bed as my thighs tighten around his head. I thread my fingers through his silky hair. His tongue ring hitting my sensitive nub increases the pleasure. He devours my pussy until rapture consumes my entire being.

I bite my bottom lip as shivers overtake my body. My eyes slowly open.

"Art," I moan, as the last tremors subsides.

It's not a dream. A naked Art is in my bedroom, his head between my legs, lapping at my pussy.

"Art, what are you doing?" I whisper.

He lifts his head. "I told you I'd be waiting for you when you got back."

"No, we can't let this happen again. Please leave."

"If you don't give me what I want, I'll take it. Did you really think one night of fucking you would be enough for me? You're not stupid. You knew I'd be coming back for more."

God help me, because damn if I don't want more of him.

He kisses my stomach, pushing my T-shirt up to dip his tongue in my navel. Once he's had his fill, he licks his way up my body to explore my breasts. He sucks my left nipple into his warm mouth while lightly pinching the other until it becomes a hard point. Art's free hand ventures to my cunt to glide his fingers through the creamy wetness there. His finger travels to my rectum to penetrate my virgin ass. The lubricated digit slides in easily. My body undulates under him. I trail kisses across his forehead. He roughly flips me over. His large body covers my back—his substantial weight pressing me into the mattress. He positions the broad head of his penis at my entrance. I make soft mewling noises as he slowly works his way into my still sore pussy. He doesn't start off fast and furious like the first time, but still the effect is just as profound. Art's big dick stretches me so deliciously. This boy is so fucking intoxicating to my senses. We moan in unison when he fills me to the brim.

"Two fucking weeks, and you're already under my fucking skin," Art growls in my ear. "How the fuck did you do that?" he asks, thoroughly confused.

I whimper when he bites my neck, causing a stinging pain. I know he broke skin. Art cannot give me pleasure without first inflicting pain. He entwines his fingers with mine and takes possession of my mouth, kissing me with an intensity that leaves me dizzy. He pulls out of me, then rams back in, balls deep. My soaked pussy makes wet sounds with every agonizingly slow move forward.

"You make me forget, and you make me want," he says angrily.

"My life was perfect before you came here. You ruined everything," I return with my own anger.

"That's our fate then. We'll ruin each other." He captures my lips again.

His fucking becomes barbaric, like a sudden madness overtakes him. He makes me feel… He makes me feel explosive. He's the match, and I'm the fuse.

"Art, stop, we're making too much noise."

His pace doesn't falter, instead it increases tenfold.

"Josh will hear us."

"Fuck him."

My mind-blowing climax leaves me a puddle of nerves. I bite into the mattress to muffle my screams. He sounds like a wild animal as his teeth dig into my shoulder. The noises he emits are unintelligible. He fucks me with wild abandon until he finally shudders, then goes lax. His heavy weight is comforting. When he's composed enough, he slips from my body, gets dressed, and leaves my bedroom without a word.

CHAPTER twenty one

ART

Fucking shit, I can't get enough of her. I'm completely reckless when it comes to Cin. I waited until midnight to silently make my way upstairs to her bedroom. I was afraid her door would be locked, but the fact it wasn't was like an open invitation. I watched her sleep for a few minutes before stripping out of my clothes. I didn't know how she would react to my presence in her bedroom, but she didn't fight me. Instead, she accepted me. Fuck, her pussy is therapeutic. I have no idea if she's on birth control, and I never asked. I really need to ask her about that. There's absolutely no way I want to bring a kid into my fucked-up life. I wouldn't know how to be a good father. Common sense evaporated the moment my dick slid inside her pussy. Releasing my cum into her warm wetness transported me to paradise. I could fuck her every night and never get enough of her delectable body. But after being in her paradise, my mind took me to a dark place as I slumbered. My escape in Cin will always be temporary.

She was already gone by the time I left for school. My eyes continuously wander to the entrance of the classroom door, waiting her arrival like some pussy-whipped bitch. Fuck it, Cin does have the best pussy I've ever had, so maybe I am addicted to it.

My classmates saunter into the room with gloomy faces, dragging their feet, pissed off because it's Monday morning again. Most of them are hung over as fuck. Finally, Cin enters the classroom with Trevor. I smirk when my eyes land on their entwined hands—*aww, how sweet*. If only he knew my dick was buried in her pussy for the last two days. Cin's frantic eyes seek me out. She's a nervous wreck. My smirk turns into a smile. I like to see her squirm. She doesn't know what to expect from me. Will I tell Trevor or not? That's the question running through her mind right now, even though I already told her I wouldn't and I won't—at least not for now. I openly watch her, even as they take their seats in their usual spots.

"Stop staring at my fucking girlfriend," Trevor demands.

"I can't. She looks good enough to eat."

"That's it, motherfucker." Trevor jumps up.

Cin is right behind him, clutching his arm, trying to stop him. I left my chair to meet him halfway the moment he stood. I'm not going to let him get the jump on me. We're in each other's faces now.

"It's about time you get knocked down a few pegs," Trevor says.

"And you're the one that's going to do it? You better ask your friends about me. They know I fuck bitches up."

"Trevor, don't." Cin looks petrified.

"Fight!" someone shouts.

Mr. Beck walks into the classroom. "Trevor and Art, is there a problem? This is the second time I've found you two at each other's throats."

"I'm merely admiring Cin here." I nod my head towards her. "But I don't think Trevor appreciates the compliment."

"Trevor?" Mr. Beck looks at him.

"I'm good."

"Then all of you sit down. The next time I see you two like this, I'm going to call your parents and we can have a discussion in the principal's office." When Mr. Beck turns his back to walk to the front of the classroom, I blow Trevor a kiss just to dig my claws further into his skin. His body goes rigid. Man, he's pissed.

"Come on, Trevor." Cin pulls him back to their desks.

I wasn't overexaggerating when I said she looks good enough to eat. I can't wait to fuck her tonight.

Cin

I've been tense all day, more so now since Trevor is walking me to the next class I have with Art. He insists on walking me to this particular class every day. I didn't know what to expect from Art today, but he kept his mouth shut like he said he would. Bri sat with him at lunch and was all over him, to Lilah's dismay. I wasn't too pleased either. I wonder if Art feels the same way when he sees me with Trevor. I found myself thinking about what it would be like if Art were my boyfriend. Maybe I'm attracted to his damage. That's the only way I can explain this madness. Could I really leave Trevor to be with him? Art is a wild card, unpredictable and dangerous. Trevor and I have a history, and he's safe. I'm not ready to let him go, or the future we have planned together. I think Dex and Zeke have a newfound respect for Art since he didn't rat them out. Of course, Josh, Robbie, Aiden, Danny, and Trevor still hate him. It would take an act of God for them to change how they feel about him.

"Do you like the attention Art gives you?" Trevor asks.

"Where did that question come from?"

"You never have my back when it comes to him. We're supposed to be a team."

"Trevor, we are a team. I don't want you to get into trouble. Can't you ignore him? Why is that so hard?"

"You want me to be the bigger person?"

"Yes. What's wrong with that?"

"It makes me look like a pathetic wimp. That's what's wrong. He stares at my girl like he wants to fuck her, but I'm supposed to pretend like I don't see it."

"Staring isn't a crime."

"Why do you sit beside him in trigonometry?"

"I don't. He sits beside me."

"Then move."

"I have, but he follows me."

"Tell the teacher he's harassing you."

"I can deal with him."

"I don't want you to deal with him!" Trevor yells, drawing a few gazes.

"I don't want to argue, so drop it." I walk ahead of him.

"I'm sorry for yelling."

"Go to class."

I fortify myself before walking through the door. I avoid eye contact with Art and sit at a desk in the middle of the classroom, as far away from him as possible. Just like I knew he would, Art moves from the desk in the back to sit at the empty one next to me.

"You like when I chase you, don't you?"

"Why do you like to provoke Trevor?"

"His reaction entertains me."

"This isn't a joke," I snap.

"Turn to chapter three in your textbook. Complete the first two pages. Keep in mind there will be a quiz on Friday." Mr. Hall sits behind his desk and starts typing away on his laptop.

I take a pencil, paper, and textbook from my backpack to begin the assignment.

"Your pussy is the sweetest thing I have ever tasted. I want more," Art whispers in my ear as he leans over the desk.

His words make me instantly horny.

"You have to stay away from me." He makes me so damn weak.

"Why didn't you lock your bedroom door?"

"What?"

"If you wanted me to stay away, you would've locked your door. You knew damn well I was going to come to your bedroom, right where you wanted me."

Maybe he's right. Maybe I left the door unlocked because subconsciously I wanted him to come.

I never should've gone down this route with him. I'm going to spin out of control eventually.

"Are you on birth control?"

"Yes."

"Good, because tonight when the house is quiet, I'm going to creep up to your bedroom and ram my dick inside your tight pussy."

CHAPTER twenty two

Cin

I think about the events over the last few weeks while I eat a bowl of cereal at the dining room table. Art has visited my bedroom for the last three nights, and like the slut I'm becoming, I've welcomed him with open arms. It's almost like I've known him my whole life. Art left my bedroom on Sunday right after he came, but lately he stays with me until dawn. Not even the fear of being caught prompts me to deny him. During the night, I'm transported to a dreamland, but when the sun rises, I crash back to reality. I always fall asleep in his arms, but he remains awake. He avoids sleep like the plague in an attempt to elude his demons, but he's only human, so eventually his body shuts down, seeking the rest it needs. He tosses and turns, his body drenched in sweat and his face wet with tears from his battle with his subconscious. The first night, he pushed me away when I tried to console him, but in his vulnerable state, he couldn't fight me off for long. I held him and after a while, he let down his guard, holding on to me like a lifeline.

"Tell me about Cole."

Art's head rests in my lap as my fingertips run along the beautiful tattoo of his brother. I was in awe of the image when I first laid eyes on it.

He didn't respond for so long, I thought he wouldn't answer.

"He was amazing."

I wipe the tears from his face. "What did he like to do?"

He gives a small smile. "He loved books about cars. He begged me to read at bedtime mostly every night. He loved all the Marvel characters too."

"Who was his favorite?"

"The Hulk. He called him the Green Giant. Green became his favorite color."

"Art?"

"Yeah?"

"Can I ask you something?" *I know this question might set him off, but I'm compelled to ask it anyway.*

"It's a free country."

"Have you ever been to Cole's gravesite?"

"Not since the day he was buried."
"You should visit."
"No."
"It could help you to—"
"Do you not understand fucking English? I said no."
He leaves the bed, searching for his scattered clothes.
"Where are you going?"
"You don't know when to shut the fuck up, Cin."
"I'm sorry, okay? Please don't go," I said, standing.
I grab his face to bring his lips to mine. He pushes me back onto the bed. We spoke no more of his brother that night.

It's been difficult to function at school due to lack of sleep. My family, friends, and most importantly Trevor notice I haven't been my usual self. We don't have sex as much, so he's starting to wonder if he did something wrong. I don't recognize myself anymore. This isn't me, but I'm not ready for what Art and I have to be over.

"Morning," Josh says in greeting, sitting in the chair opposite me. He drops his glass of milk and breakfast burrito on the table.

I was so lost in my thoughts I didn't hear when the door opened.

"Morning," I reply, distracted.

"What is up with you, Cin?"

"Nothing. I'm fine." I look down, pretending to be interested in my soggy cereal.

"You're not. You've been walking around with your head in the clouds all week."

"I said I'm fine."

"Sorry for trying to see what's been bugging my almost stepsister," he replies defensively. "I'm tired of Trevor asking me about you."

I jerk my head up. "What did he say?"

"He's just trying to figure out what the hell he did to make you switch up all of a sudden. Since he's been over here every night this week, I thought things were cool between you two."

"Huh?"

"You know," he whispers. "His nightly visits."

"Oh, right."

He gives me a "what the hell did you think I was talking about" look.

"I've been meaning to rip into his ass about all the noise you guys make." He takes a drink of his milk.

"No!" I yell.

My outburst causes him to choke on his milk, spilling most of it on his clothes.

"Jesus. Now I have to change."

"Sorry," I grumble. "There's no need to talk to him about the noise. We'll keep it down."

"Whatever."

Art bumps into him as he leaves the dining room.

"Watch where the fuck you're going," he growls.

Art's response is to give him the finger.

"Hi," I say shyly.

"Don't play coy now. You're a wildcat when I'm between your legs."

"Be quiet. Someone could hear you." I glance towards the door, expecting Josh to come barging in.

My cell phone chimes.

Trevor: I'm outside.

Me: Coming.

"I have to go."

Before I can make a move, Art stands behind my chair and yanks my ponytail back painfully.

"Is that your boyfriend?"

"Let go. That hurts," I whimper.

"You play house with your fucking boyfriend during the day, but remember who owns your pussy at night."

Art kisses me then… no, it's a branding. His tongue licks every inch of my mouth before letting me go.

"Now, go run along." He grips my pussy. "You keep this warm and wet for me today."

It's going to be a long ride to school.

"Cin, I wish you would talk to me," Trevor pleads from the driver's seat of his Jeep.

"Trevor—"

"Please don't lie to me. We've always been open with each other. If I did something wrong, tell me. I promise to fix it, babe. I want you to be happy."

God, he's sweet, caring, and loving—so why do I crave Art like he's my reason for existing?

Tears run down my cheeks.

"Don't cry, babe."

"I'm sorry I haven't been myself. I have a lot on my mind."

"Tell me." He squeezes my knee.

"It's just graduating high school and attending college is a big step," I say lamely.

"That's it? Don't worry. I'll be there with you."

"What happens if you don't get accepted?"

"If I don't, I'll still be nearby."

"You're right. I'm being stupid."

"It's all good, babe. At first, I thought maybe Art had something to do with your mood change."

"Why would you think that?" I ask nonchalantly.

"Your attitude has gradually shifted since he moved here."

"It has nothing to do with him."

Liar.

"You sure?"

"Of course." I'm surprised I wasn't struck by a bolt of lightning.

"We usually fuck like rabbits, unable to keep our hands off each other."

"I know."

"I miss being inside you. Can I come over tonight?"

"Not tonight. Friday, okay?"

"Remember when we broke up?"

"Yeah."

"I never want to go through that again. Not being with you isn't an option for me. I love you, Cin."

"I love you too."

"What the fuck?" Anneli screams.

I lean over, clutching my knees, attempting to catch my breath. "I'm trying my best!"

I've spent the last half hour aiming to beat my winning time from last track season, but to no avail. In fact, it's a lot worse. Our coach is tough. If I come to first practice in this shape, she's going to be on my ass.

"Your best isn't good enough!"

"Fuck you!"

"Fuck you too!"

"Bitch." I walk off the track field.

"If you continue running like that, you won't make it to Regionals or State this year," she yells at my back.

"I know."

"Don't give me that bullshit you've been feeding to everybody else. I want to know what's really going on, and I want to know right now," she demands.

I drop to my knees, my guilt and lack of sleep catching up with me. Anneli is at my side in a heartbeat.

"I'm sorry for being hard on you. It's my job to make sure you don't give up, to push you to your limit and beyond. If I didn't, I wouldn't be much of a friend. I know you're better than this."

My uncontrollable sobs make it difficult to breathe. "I cheated on Trevor," I say between deep breaths.

"Why would you do that?"

"Because I'm the bitch I just called you."

"End it, and don't tell Trevor," Anneli suggests.

If only it were that simple. "I can't."

"Yes, you can."

"It's Art."

"Holy shit. You go and fuck the one guy your boyfriend hates. That's the stupidest thing you could've ever done."

"I think I'm falling for him. He's hurting so bad. I just want to help him," I admit.

"Listen to yourself. You barely know him, and you're far from capable of helping him. Jesus, he tried to kill himself."

"It's like we're connected on a visceral level. I can't help it. I know it's wrong, but I can't stop."

"This is not going to end well. Imagine what Trevor will do if he finds out."

Am I prepared for the repercussions that will surely come if I continue down this path?

"Who do you see a future with? Art is just a thrill for you, something different and exciting, an infatuation that will pass. If you think he's the type to want a steady girlfriend, you're deluding yourself."

I can't dispute what she's saying. It's the truth. Staying home tonight isn't an option. I need time to collect my thoughts.

"Can I spend the night at your house?"

"Of course you can."

I can't be in the same house with Art tonight.

Lorrain Allen

CHAPTER twenty three

ART

One day without being inside her, and I'm losing my fucking mind. What has this girl done to me? She came home after school yesterday, only to go back out within minutes. I swear if I had her cell phone number, I would've texted her to demand that she come home. There's no way I could ask Josh for it—he would've told me to fuck off. More than a few times, I found myself almost heading upstairs to ask my uncle for her number. Each time, I stopped myself. Now it's Friday night, and she hasn't come home yet. In class this morning, she pretended like I didn't exist. Her eyes never strayed my way—not one damn time. Even Trevor ignored the snide remarks I tossed their way. I didn't realize how much I craved her attention until she took it from me.

Bri sat with me at lunch and talked nonstop the entire time. I declined her invitation to come over to her house later tonight. If I were smart, I would forget about Cin and just fuck Bri—maybe fuck her cousin too while I'm at it—but it's Cin who calms my mind. I can't forget the paradise I found with her in the middle of a raging storm. Bri told me about a small get-together she's having on Saturday night. I accepted that invite, only because Cin will be there.

She skipped the afternoon class we have together. She's fucked up if she thinks I'm going to allow her to walk away from me. I was dormant until she came along and woke me up, so now it's her responsibility to feed me. I silently seethe while lying on her bed as I wait in the darkness. Even the risk of being seen didn't stop me from coming to her room. I amble over to the window when I hear the engine of a car. I peer through the small opening in the curtain, careful not to make my presence known. My dick gets hard instantly as my eyes greedily track her when she leaves her car, then disappears up the porch steps. It's close to ten o'clock. I've been waiting on her for close to an hour. I quickly stride over to the door and lean against the wall—a lion waiting on its prey to unknowingly venture into dangerous territory. She'll have a false sense of security when she enters her bedroom, never expecting the threat that lies within. I'll strike hard and fast when she steps through the door. She won't know what hit her.

I pounce on her when she clears the doorway, covering her mouth when she takes a breath to scream. My nails dig into the soft skin of her face, not enough to draw blood but enough to leave grooves. She claws at me like a wildcat when my forearm slides across her throat. My girl, Cin, is a fighter. My dick just got harder. I kick the door closed.

"Where the fuck you been?"

The fight in her vanishes when she hears my voice. That was her second mistake. She should never let her guard down around me. Her first mistake was thinking I wouldn't be waiting for her to fuck us both to unconsciousness.

Cin

A million thoughts race through my mind the moment I am attacked. I am ambushed before I can switch on the light.

The few seconds of the unknown felt like a lifetime, then his voice washes over me like a warm caress. I attempt to speak, but my words are mumbled. The adrenaline gradually dissipates from my limbs, leaving me weak. His hand glides from my mouth to knot in my long locks.

"Art," I croak.

"Shut the fuck up."

I cry out when my hair is savagely yanked back. My starving lungs are flooded with much-needed oxygen after Art removes his arm from across my neck. He guides me forward by the tight grip he has on my hair. He follows me to the floor as he forces me to my knees at the side of the bed. My head is roughly pushed into the mattress. Though he only holds me down by one hand, I'm no match for his strength. Art grinds his massive hard-on against my ass.

"You can't escape me, but the truth is, you don't want to anyway," he whispers in my ear.

A tree wouldn't want to escape the sun because it'll die without it. He's my fucking sun. Trevor is my heart, but Art is becoming my soul. I expected his punishment the moment I walked through the front door and was yearning for it. I promised Anneli I was done with Art, that I recognize he'll always be a restless spirit in search of absolution that will forever be out of his reach. A restless spirit's nature is to bring destruction to those around it.

"It's the truth, isn't it? You're hungry for me." His lips move against my cheek as he speaks.

"You take me on a natural high I never want to come down from."

"Then let's get high together."

Art frantically tugs my sweatpants and panties to mid-thigh, then pulls out his manhood before savagely impaling me. We both moan at the exquisiteness of his breadth expanding my center to uncomfortable measures bordering on pain. He fucks me unrestrained, swiftly rolling his hips to feed my famished cunt. The wildness in him takes over, causing him to appear more beast claiming his woman than human as he snarls. I'm scared the sound of us having sex is loud enough to possibly draw the attention of Ricky and my mom, who are home. Josh isn't home, since his car isn't outside. Thank God.

"You crave me just as much as I crave you." He cranes my head to the side and seizes my lips in a violent kiss.

We swallow each other's energy as he takes ownership of my body, tilting my entire being on its axis, taking me past the heavens into unchartered space.

The wonderful bliss wrapped around me is interrupted by a tap at my bedroom window.

Oh my God, it's Trevor. I forgot I told him he could come over tonight.

I begin to struggle. "Stop, it's Trevor."

"No. He has to wait his turn."

"Art, please."

His answer is to pump his hips brutally, obliterating my soft folds. My hands twist into the sheets as his dick continues to conquer the depths of my pussy.

The tapping gets louder. I would've been caught red-handed if it weren't for my curtains.

My pussy begins to contract, transporting me to ecstasy at warp speed. I bite my wrist to keep from screaming out. Before I know what's happening, Art stands, then mercilessly snatches my hair back and comes all over my face. He jerks his length at rapid speed until the last of his cum has been released. I'm in shock at his actions, but what he does next is beyond belief. He smears his cum across my face and down my neck.

"Now when he kisses you, he'll taste me."

When he lets go of my hair, I turn slightly to watch him from my position on the floor. He stuffs his still-hard dick back into his pants. He leaves my bedroom without sparing me another look. I remain where I am, in a trance until the sound of knocking draws my attention. I take off my hoodie, leaving me in my tank top, to clean my face and neck of Art's semen, but I'm still sticky. I stand, taking my sweatpants off to throw in the dirty clothes hamper with my soiled hoodie. I unlock and open the window. I step back as Trevor climbs through.

"Why were you ignoring me?"

"I wasn't."

"I called and texted you over a dozen times."

My cell phone was in my hand when Art rushed me.

I walk over to the door to feel along the floor until I find my phone. I don't dare turn on the light—afraid of what my appearance may give away. "I must've dropped it."

Trevor wraps his arms around me. "You're soaking wet."

I pull away. "I'm just a little hot."

I move to walk past him, but he latches onto my arm, trying to bring me in for a kiss that I quickly avoid.

"What's the matter?"

"Bad breath. I ate some pasta that was loaded with garlic. I have to brush my teeth. I'll be right back."

When I leave my bedroom, I'm ambushed for the second time that night.

"Art, what are you doing?" I ask in a low voice.

He drags me into the bathroom before closing the door. "I'm not done yet."

"No."

"Yes."

"Trevor is waiting for me," I whisper.

"I don't give a fuck."

"Please, can you at least lock the door?"

He gives me a hard stare but does what I ask. "First, you're going to suck your cream off my dick."

Art savagely rips my panties off before forcing me to sit on the closed toilet.

He taps his dick on my lips. "Open wide."

The only way to avoid detection is to do what he wants. He won't let me leave until I do. His dick plunges down my throat, causing me to throw up a little. My eyes water, and I continuously gag as he relentlessly thrusts into my mouth.

His head falls back. "Ahh shit."

He pulls his dick from my mouth, then drops it to between my open thighs. My arms and legs encircle him as he fills me up. I lay my head on his shoulder as he takes me on another ride to the heights of pleasure.

The doorknob jiggles. "What are you doing?"

Trevor's voice doesn't stop Art's assault on my pussy.

"I need a few more minutes," I respond.

"Are you okay?"

"Yes. Please go back to my bedroom before Ricky and my mom hear you."

"Okay. Hurry up."

Art bites down on my ear as we come together.

"He can have you now," Art says, slipping his dick from my ravaged cunt.

I hold my breath when he opens the bathroom door, praying that Trevor went back to my bedroom like I told him to. My nerves ease when he doesn't appear in the doorway. Art glances over his shoulder to stare between my spread legs where cum seeps from my hole to pool on the toilet.

"When he feasts on your cunt, he'll taste me there too," he says before leaving.

I shut the door and take a shower before facing my boyfriend.

Trevor knows to lock the bedroom door since sometimes my mom will barge right in, so I lightly knock.

"It's me, Trevor," I whisper.

I wrapped the ruined panties in my tank top. I'll get rid of them later.

"You were gone longer than a few minutes," Trevor says in annoyance as he opens the door.

His tirade ends when he sees me standing there in a tiny towel.

He jerks me into the room, then closes the door. The towel is ripped from my body before I'm thrown on the bed. Trevor lands on top of me, attacking my breasts with vigor. He pulls his pants down just enough for his hard dick to spring free and cruelly push inside my cunt.

"Be gentle," I caution.

My pussy is a wreck after Art. My behavior is beyond irresponsible. I never thought I'd be the type of girl to have unprotected sex with two boys in the same night.

"I'm sorry. I'll go slowly."

He gently rocks his hips until his erection is completely embedded in my vagina. He makes love to me, unhurriedly pumping between my legs. He gives me the sweetest lingering kisses. Trevor's fucking is the opposite of Art's, more like a gentle breeze on a beautiful beach. Art's fucking is more like a volcano, hot and dangerous. A throbbing starts in my center before dissipating as I reach the crescendo of my climax. My shuddering cunt triggers Trevor's orgasm. He groans as his cum spills inside me.

CHAPTER twenty four

Cin

I wake up to Ricky calling my name through my bedroom door.

"Come in," I grumble.

"Good morning," Ricky says in greeting.

"Morning." I yawn.

"We need to talk. Can you come to the dining room in ten minutes?" Ricky asks.

"Okay."

Fuck. Does he know about Art and me? How could he? Well, we were a bit loud last night.

Josh and I walk downstairs together.

"What does your dad want?"

"Hell if I know, but I don't appreciate being woken up this early on a Saturday morning."

I'm on pins and needles as Josh and I enter the dining room. Ricky sits in his usual chair at the head of the table. Art isn't here, so maybe I'm being paranoid. If Ricky wanted to confront us, I'm sure my mom would be involved and Art would be present, not Josh. Also, Ricky doesn't have a look of disappointment on his face. In fact, he actually appears pretty happy, sporting a goofy grin.

"What's so important you couldn't wait until a decent hour to tell us?" Josh asks, crossing his arms.

I glance expectantly at Ricky before taking a seat. "Why isn't my mom here? What's with the secrecy?"

Ricky places a small open box featuring a beautiful engagement ring on the table.

"Oh my God!"

"Keep quiet, Cin. You'll give away the surprise." Ricky smiles.

"Is that it? I'm going back to bed," Josh says.

"Stay where you are."

I jump up in excitement, run over to Ricky, and give him a big hug. "Congratulations."

"Thanks."

"Are you sure you want to propose? I mean, why buy the cow when you can get the milk for free?" Josh asks.

"Why do you have to be such an asshole and ruin this moment?" I ask.

No more shacking up for my mom and Ricky. I'm happy this day has finally come.

"I thought you would be happy for us."

"If you have to get married, I guess Missy is okay."

"When do you plan to propose?" I ask.

"At her birthday party, so family and friends can witness the special event."

I'm not a party planner, so while I know about the surprise party, I won't be helping with anything. Katrina and Ricky have everything under control.

"Well, congrats. I'm going back to bed," Josh says, leaving the dining room.

"I couldn't ask for a more awesome stepdad."

"That means a lot to me."

At least the new year is looking up for my mom, even though it's filled with uncertainty for me.

ART

As I approach Bri's house, I notice Dex on the porch, lounging in a chair.

"Hey, man."

I walk up the steps without returning his greeting.

"It's okay to acknowledge the existence of others."

"I'm not your friend, and I don't want you to be."

"I know that. I wanted to say I'm sorry about your brother. I know how it feels."

"You don't know shit."

"My cousin drowned."

I glance towards him. Is this motherfucker pulling my leg? If he is, I'm going to beat his ass. "Don't fuck with me."

"I wouldn't joke about something like this. We were both twelve when he drowned at the beach. We were so competitive—always challenging and daring each other. We decided to see who could swim the farthest and fastest. We'd done it a million times before, but this time the outcome was different. He disappeared underneath the waves, and I couldn't find him. I spiraled out of control after that day, so my family relocated from California to here for a fresh start a few months later. What's fucked up most of all is that his body was never found. I never told my friends about him."

"Why are you telling me this?"

"To let you know it does get better. The pain never goes away, but it gets a little easier each day."

"It'll never get easier for me."

"It will. Just take it one day at a time."

I nod, then walk inside the house. The usual people sit around the living room, but one person has my complete attention. The object of my obsession graces the lap of her boyfriend. She's a tomboy in every sense of the word, but still the sexiest girl in this room. Shit, the sexiest girl in the whole damn school.

"Art, I'm so glad you came." Bri appears at my side, grasps my forearm, and pulls me over to the loveseat. Beer bottles, Patrón, and shot glasses litter the coffee table.

"You're the only one," Aiden grumbles.

"I'm happy you're here too, Art." Lilah winks.

"You're just in time for a game of Truth or Dare." Bri tugs me down to sit beside her.

"I'm not interested in playing a stupid ass child's game."

"Come on. It'll be fun. Anyway, since you're here, you have to join in." Lilah sips her beer.

"Maybe after the game, you, Lilah, and I can go to my bedroom for a little fun," Bri murmurs in my ear.

"Are we playing the game or what?" Danny takes a puff of his joint. "You want to take a hit? Oh, I'm sorry, I forgot, you prefer cocaine." He laughs.

"Shut up, Danny," Bri hisses.

"You can talk all the shit you want, but you're no match against me in a fistfight."

"No fighting, guys," Bri snaps.

"Then rein in your dog," Robbie says.

The assholes laugh like that's the funniest joke they've ever heard.

"Danny talked shit first as always. I'm tired of all this drama. Just start the fucking game," Cin says, effectively shutting down the argument before it can escalate further.

My girl always defends me.

My girl? Where the hell did that come from?

"I'll go first," Robbie volunteers. "Anneli, truth or dare?"

"So, we're playing this game tonight," Dex says, entering the living room.

"You would choose me, prick," Anneli grumbles.

"Yep, that's me, Mr. Prick." Robbie chuckles.

"Dare."

"Oh, you shouldn't have chosen that." Robbie rubs his hands together.

"Wait, I change my mind," Anneli says in alarm.

Dex laughs as he sits on the settee. "You know that's not going to fly."

"You can't change your mind," Bri says.

"Why not?"

Aiden chimes in. "It's against the rules."

"There are no rules for truth or dare," Anneli huffs.

"If you refuse, you have to take a shot." Lilah pours Patrón into a shot glass.

"Patrón is gross."

"Well, if you don't want to take a shot, you know what to do," Josh says.

"Fine. Lay it on me."

"I dare you to kiss Zeke." Robbie smirks.

The room goes deathly silent as Zeke's eyes light up. He must have a thing for Anneli. I hadn't noticed before.

"No."

Lilah holds out the shot glass. "Drink."

Anneli cringes. "Okay. I'll do it."

Zeke eagerly leaves his perch on the sectional to approach Anneli. Her nervousness is clearly visible in the change of her breathing and her inability to sit still. He clutches her wrist and hauls her forward into his body before latching his lips to hers for a searing kiss. His hands slide around her body to grip her ample ass. Anneli resists at first but melts into his embrace.

Clapping and whistling resounds throughout the living room.

Anneli ends the kiss, pushing at his chest to get away. "Enough!"

"It'll never be enough." He captures her mouth again.

She turns her head, struggling vehemently. "Zeke, stop."

"Let her go," Dex says.

Anneli manages to break free, then races from the room with Zeke in pursuit.

"Well, that was rather entertaining," Robbie says.

"I'll go next," I say, surprising everyone in the room. "Cin, truth or dare?"

The look on her face is priceless, the rabbit caught by the fox. Trevor stiffens as he prepares for what will happen next.

"Truth," she replies meekly.

"Is it true you never cheated on Trevor?"

"Motherfucker! Cin would never cheat on me!" Trevor's outburst nearly knocks Cin from his lap.

"You never know. Maybe she has a taste for some new dick," I taunt.

When Trevor tries to remove Cin from his lap, she wraps her arms around him to hinder his movement.

"No, you promised," Cin pleads.

"It's about time someone put this motherfucker in his place."

"Calm down, it's only a game. Cin, you have to answer the question," Bri says.

"No, I've never cheated on Trevor." She doesn't even flinch when the lie leaves her mouth.

"And she never would," Trevor says.

If only the bastard knew.

"Truth or dare?" Danny asks me, snuffing his joint out in an ashtray.

If they think the game has been entertaining this far, the encore is going to be epic.

"Truth."

"Is it true you tried to kill yourself?"

"Man, that's fucked up," Dex says.

"Danny, that's not cool," Cin says in disgust.

"Yep," I answer.

"You must be some kind of fucked up to want to off yourself." Danny shakes his head.

"Shut up," Bri hisses.

"Truth or dare?" Danny asks again.

Lilah interjects. "Hey, you had your turn."

"Dare."

Danny stands, pulling a pocketknife from his pants. He pulls the sharp blade from the enclosure before tossing it in the air and catching it at the handle.

"I dare you to finish the job."

"You're taking this too far," Josh says.

"I'm only offering him the chance to put an end to his suffering. You want to die right? Here, let me help you." He grabs my arm, sliding the blade along my wrist.

I quickly stand, pushing him away. "Get your fucking hands off me."

"I can't believe you did that! He's bleeding!" Cin shouts.

Josh and Robbie jump to their feet, preparing to intervene if necessary. Zeke and Anneli walk back into the living room after hearing the commotion.

"You're nothing but a chickenshit," Danny snickers.

"Let's see who the real chickenshit is. It's time for Chaos," I say.

"Bring it, motherfucker. I'm up for anything you throw my way," Danny says in challenge.

"Truth or Dare is child's play. It's time for the big leagues. Are you up for a game of Chicken?"

"Are you insane?" Cin asks.

"A little bit."

"Someone could die," Robbie says.

"It's a nice night for a drive. Follow me to Fox Road. It's practically empty at this hour." Danny leaves the house.

Josh blocks my path when I go to follow.

"This is stupid."

"I'll go right the fuck through you," I threaten.

"Don't let him leave," Cin says in a trembling voice.

"No, let him go since he's so big and bad," Trevor says.

Cin shoots him a death glare.

"Move out of my way."

"Fine, it'll be your funeral."

I brush past Josh, straight to my motorcycle.

Cin

I grip the handle of Art's bike. "Wait!"

"Back off," he says.

"Don't do this."

Trevor clasps me around the waist to forcibly remove me. Art starts the engine, then zooms down the street.

"I can't believe you're letting this happen."

"Do you honestly think anyone can stop him when he sets his mind to do something?" Trevor asks.

"Chill, Cin. Danny isn't a psycho. He'll chicken out at the last second," Bri assures me.

"And Art is?" I ask.

"Well, yeah," Bri says.

"We're going to miss the action!" Lilah exclaims.

"This is a serious situation, and that's all you can say?" Anneli asks.

"It's not too late to put a stop to this madness." I run towards Trevor's truck, jumping in the passenger seat. "Come on!" I yell over my shoulder.

Once Anneli, Lilah, and Bri pile into the back seat, Trevor speeds down the road. Everyone else has already left. By the time we make it to the destination of tonight's fuckery, the opponents are positioned at opposite ends on the road.

"It's too late," I say.

We're out of the truck in seconds to join the rest of the group in a grassy area on the side of the road.

They take off when Aiden lifts his fist in the air. I don't think I've ever been this scared in my life. Smoke billows as the wheels of Art's motorcycle spin on the concrete. My eyes are riveted on him. Though the scene before me unfolds in slow motion, it only takes moments for them to reach each other. Danny jerks his Mustang to the left at the last possible second, clipping the end of the bike. I scream when the Mustang crashes into a tree and Art is flung from his motorcycle. His body rolls across the pavement along with the motorcycle creating bright sparks illuminating the darkness as it slides sideways down the asphalt. Lilah and Bri follow me over to Art while the rest check on Danny. Art pushes himself to a sitting position, so maybe he isn't hurt too badly. I notice that his face is covered in abrasions when I kneel at his side.

"You fucking moron! You could've been killed!" I shout.

Blood trickles from his mouth. "Would you care if I was?"

Bri laughs. The bitch actually laughs. "I knew you wouldn't let Danny show you up."

I tackle her to the ground in a blind rage. We roll across the ground, pulling hair and slapping at each other. Trevor drags me off of her, gripping tightly to prevent further attack while Josh holds Bri back.

"What the fuck is your issue?" she screams.

"You are."

"We have to get Danny to a hospital. He's hurt really bad," Dex says.

Damn, I forgot about him. A groaning Danny is being held up by Aiden and Zeke. His arm dangles at an odd angle and his face is a bloody mess.

"We are so fucked. How are we going to explain this?" Robbie yanks his hand through his hair.

"Use my truck to drive the girls to Bri's house," Josh orders me. "Trevor, we'll use your truck to take Danny to the hospital. We can think of a lie on the way."

Bri jerks her arm away from Josh before stomping to the truck and slamming the door closed once she's inside.

"Do you need to go to the hospital?" Josh grudgingly asks Art.

"Fuck off."

"Fine, it'd be nice if every bone in your body was broken," he grumbles, walking away.

"I'll call you later, babe," Trevor says, getting inside his truck.

He misses the glare I toss his way. I hope Danny is okay, though he brought this on himself.

"Can you walk?" I'm mad at myself for being so concerned for Art when he doesn't give a fuck.

He slowly pushes to his feet. The urge to help him beats at me, but I'm so fucking pissed at him, and I need to be careful about our interactions when others are around. My eyes roam over his body to ensure he's intact as he limps over to his motorcycle.

"That's it? You're just going to walk away?" I ask.

He stands his motorcycle up before climbing on and speeds down the road without acknowledging me. It seems the bike didn't sustain any extensive damage.

"It's obvious you didn't end it with him. You need to before it's too late," Anneli whispers.

I'm past the point of no return, so it's already too damn late.

"What did she say to you?" Lilah asks.

"Nothing, let's get out of here."

CHAPTER twenty five

Cin

I storm into the house, intent on giving Art a piece of my mind. He doesn't flinch when his bedroom door is flung open. He lounges on the bed with a bag of frozen peas covering the left side of his face. My body vibrates with anger, but when he smirks at me, I see red. I grab the bag of peas and smack him in the face with them. His hand latches onto my neck, and he slams me on the bed. His heavy body covers mine.

"I always knew you had claws but compared to me you're just a fucking cub."

"You could've been killed! You're a fucking lunatic!" My arms flail, fighting him with everything I have.

I'll never match his strength, and he proves it by capturing my wrists with one hand to pin above my head.

"Why are you crying?" he asks.

"I'm not crying."

He licks the tears from my face. "Don't cry for me. I'm not worth your tears."

I lift my head, ferociously consuming his lips, and he gives me the same energy in return. I pour all of me into our kiss, exposing my emotions and not giving a damn. He's the puppet master, and I'm the puppet being controlled by him. We tear at each other's clothes until we lie exposed, our bodies as well as our hearts. I close my eyes in pure rapture when he fills me. Art fucks me so amazingly good, like it's the last time he'll ever experience this kind of intimacy. He flips me inside out, breaking me into little pieces before putting me back together again. Grunts, moans of pleasure, and the sound of our bodies impacting float through the bedroom.

My orgasm takes over, quenching the thirst my body so desperately needs. Art follows behind me, groaning as his reaches his climax.

My head rests comfortably in Cin's lap while she cleans and applies ointment on my scrapes. We're both naked, her perfect breasts within sucking distance. Cin, in all her indignant outrage, stormed into my bedroom but forgot to close the door. We could've been caught. The way we were fucking, we wouldn't have heard anyone approaching. Afterwards, Cin was horrified when she noticed. I've never seen her move so quickly. I enjoyed the view of her heart-shaped ass. Though it's small, there's still a little jiggle. I'm afforded the opportunity to study her facial features as she concentrates on her task.

"Why are you staring at me?"

"Because you're gorgeous."

A beautiful shade of red flushes her cheeks.

"Ahh, she blushes."

"All done." She twists the cap onto the tube of ointment.

"What prompted you to dye the tips of your hair pink?" I run my fingers through the glossy strands.

She shrugs her shoulders. "I wanted to switch up my appearance, I guess."

"The color suits you."

"Thanks."

"Your belly piercing is sexy as hell."

God, her smile is as bright as the fucking sun. "You're just full of compliments tonight."

"I only give them when they're due. Does your mom know you have it?"

"Yep. She took me to get the piercing for my sixteenth birthday."

"Do you want any more piercings?"

"Maybe. It's crossed my mind a few times. What about you?"

"Nah, six piercings are enough."

"Six? I only see five—tongue, lip, nose, and both of your earlobes."

I lift up my tongue so she can see my frenulum piercing.

"Did that hurt?"

"Nope, it was a walk in the park. The old man and my mother flipped out when I came home tatted and pierced."

"Did you do it to piss them off?"

"Kind of, but I got the tattoo on my back to honor my brother."

"That's a great way to keep his memory alive."

It's becoming way too easy to confide in her.

"What does the semicolon tattoo mean?"

"That I'm a suicide survivor."

"Are you happy you're still alive?"

"Yes, because death isn't good enough for me. There's peace in death."

"I'm happy you survived. You have so much to live for."

"I wish that were true."

"It is. You—"

"What nationality is your father?" I ask quickly, hoping to end this line of conversation.

"Brazilian."

"Oh, that's where your feistiness comes from. Where is he?"

"He lives in Arizona, but he's rarely home."

"Do you ever see him?"

"Not really. He's a CDL driver, so he travels most of the time, but when I visit my grandmother, he comes home if he's able to."

"Do you have a good relationship with him?"

"I would say I do. When we do have time to spend together, he always makes sure I have a great time. What about your dad?"

"What about him?" I'm not in the mood to talk about that bastard.

"Do you have a good relationship with him?"

"No." Well shit, if I had known my question was going to lead to Cin asking about my father, I would've surely avoided it.

"Just no?"

"Yeah."

"What about your mother?"

"She's a gold-digging whore. My father is a pathetic spineless bitch with a manipulative father. Ricky got out before he could be tainted. Now drop it. I don't want to talk about them."

"Can I ask you something?"

"No."

"Before your brother died, were you planning on going to college?"

"Of course. What rich kid in his prime wouldn't want the opportunity to attend fraternity parties and fuck his way through hundreds of girls on campus?"

"Typical."

"Hey, you asked. It's not my fault if you don't like the answer."

"What major did you want to study?"

"Fuck if I know."

"Did you plan on joining the family business?"

"Hell no."

"Well, what were you going to do after college?"

"It's stupid."

"Don't say that."

"It's true. It was a dumb dream."

"No one's dream is dumb. Tell me."

"I wanted to play football professionally. It doesn't matter now though. I haven't played for years and don't have the heart for the game anymore."

"What about minor league football? You could try that."

"Drop it."

"Why?"

"Because I don't have a future, and I don't deserve one. I plan to die alone with a bottle of the strongest liquor at my side."

"Stop punishing yourself. You act as if you drowned your brother yourself."

"I might as well have."

"What do you mean?"

"That's my other secret. Do you want to hear it?"

"Yes, only if you want to share it with me."

"That night, Cole asked me to go to the pool with him." I pause to take a deep breath because this is the first time I'm telling this story to anyone.

"You don't have to talk about it if you're not ready to." Cin wipes tears from my face.

Fuck, I hadn't even realized I started crying.

"I have to tell someone."

Cin brushes my hair from my forehead before kissing it. "Okay, I'm listening."

"He wanted to play with a motorized toy boat I bought him a few days earlier."

My tears flow in earnest now. Cin will be repulsed by me once I tell her what I did.

"He kept pulling my arm, begging me, so I pushed him and told him to fuck off. I remember the look on his face. It'll be etched in my mind forever. He was so damn scared because I'd never raised my voice at him before."

"I know to you it seems that way—"

"If only I took twenty minutes to take him to the pool, he'd still be alive." I turn my face into the warmth of her stomach, muffling my cries and drenching the area in my sorrow.

"You had no idea your brother would go to the pool without you. It's not your fault. Fucked-up shit happens in the world all the time."

"His terrified face is the last look he ever gave me before God took him away. I thought God was merciful. Why didn't he spare the life of an innocent three-year-old boy? God can kiss my ass."

Now she knows the secret that's been burning a hole through my brain, and she doesn't hate me. She doesn't think I'm the worst kind of monster. I feel an undeserved sense of relief.

"No one else's words are going to help you through the battle you're going through. I can't begin to understand how you feel. You'll have to find peace within yourself. I'm so sorry about your brother."

Cin and I lie together for a little while longer with her running her fingers through my hair. Some of the weight has been lifted from my shoulders.

CHAPTER twenty six

ART

"Art. Wake up."

I roll over on the bed, pulling the covers from my face to peer at Ricky, who stands in the doorway. "Don't you knock?"

"I did, but you didn't answer."

"What do you want?"

"Come into the living room."

Shit, he must've heard about Danny. I sigh, detangling myself from the bedding to trudge behind him into the living room where Josh and Cin already sit on the sofa.

"Art, have a seat."

"What's the team meeting about this morning, and will I be getting paid overtime for attending?" I sit next to a squirming Cin.

"Danny has a broken arm and a punctured lung. It'll take him weeks to recover. I want the truth about what happened last night."

"We told you. A dog ran out in the middle of the road and Danny swerved to avoid hitting it," Josh explains.

"Yeah, that's what happened. Not all heroes wear capes. Danny risked his life to save a defenseless dog," I mock. "I for one think he deserves a medal for his bravery."

Josh breaks into laughter, then starts coughing when the look on Ricky's face becomes murderous.

"This is a serious situation! The sheriff is out for blood, especially yours, Art. He's convinced you had something to do with the car accident last night."

"Why? I had nothing to do with it."

"Your motorcycle wasn't outside when I got home, so where were you?"

"I didn't know it was a crime to go out on a Saturday night. If you must know, I went to see a movie."

"That's a convenient story. What happened to your face?"

"I fell off my motorcycle."

"On the same night Danny got into a car accident, huh?"

"Yep."

"The crash happened on Fox Road," Ricky says.

"Yeah, so?" Josh scratches his chin.

"You said everyone was meeting at Bri's house. Fox Road is half an hour in the opposite direction. Your story isn't adding up."

Josh and his dipshit friends didn't have enough brain cells to rub together to come up with an airtight story.

"We were coming back from the diner," Cin says.

That's my girl, quick on her toes.

"Fucking kids," Ricky mumbles in frustration before heading upstairs.

"You dummies couldn't come up with a better story?" I ask Josh.

"Suck a dick, you bastard."

"No, thank you, but I'm sure that's what you and your friends do in your spare time—sit in a circle, sucking each other's dicks."

"It's time I fuck you up." Josh stands.

I follow his lead. "There's nothing but space and opportunity, so what's up?"

Cin tries to squeeze between us. "No. Fighting isn't going to solve anything."

"Maybe not, but finally beating the shit out of this prick will feel fucking good," Josh says.

"Let's go." It's about time to show Josh what his friends learned the night I arrived in Longhorn County.

I follow Josh out the back door with Cin on our heels.

"No, you're cousins. You shouldn't be fighting." She jumps on my back, trying to stop me.

I pry her arms from around my neck, but she wraps her body around me like a snake.

I grasp her shoulders and shake her hard. "You can't stop this! It was bound to happen!"

She stops struggling, accepting the inevitable. Something tugs at my heartstrings when she starts crying. Shit, am I growing a conscience all of a sudden? Still, I can't let her tears sway me. This thing between Josh and me should've been settled a long time ago. I take off my shirt and throw it to the ground. The son of a bitch tackles me in the next second, and damn, this motherfucker hits hard enough for me to go airborne. My body hits the ground with a thud, causing the oxygen to leave my lungs. I shake it off, jumping to my feet. This time around, I'm prepared when he makes his next move, ducking to avoid a right hook. I deliver a jab to his kidney, followed by an elbow to his nose. Blood immediately oozes from the mangled cartilage.

"You broke my fucking nose!" He wipes the liquid pouring from his nostrils.

"Now you and Zeke can be twinsies—" My lip splits the moment his fist connects with my mouth.

After that, punches fly and blood flows as we beat each other to a pulp.

"Enough!" Cin says, sobbing.

We both collapse to the ground in exhaustion. I'm sure the fight only lasted less than ten minutes, but damn, it felt like hours. Josh is a fucking asshole, but I have to give him props because he's a damn good fighter, unlike his friends. He almost whooped my ass.

"I won the fight," I say between breaths.

"Like hell. I won fair and square," Josh says.

I turn to Cin. "Who do you think won?"

"Fuck you both." She stomps off in anger.

Cin

They nearly killed each other. I drive to Lilah's house, infuriated. There's no way I could look at either one of them today without wanting to scratch their eyeballs out, so I showered and left. Of course, Ricky will want to know what happened when he sees their puffy black-and-blue faces. I park my car, then call Lilah several times before she answers.

"Hello," she growls.

"Open the door."

"You're here?"

"Duh, now open the damn door."

"All right, you don't have to be a bitch about it," she grumbles.

I impatiently wait for her on the porch while she takes her sweet time to come downstairs.

"About damn time," I say when the front door finally opens.

"I need coffee."

"You and me both." I follow her through the house to the kitchen.

"Why are you here?" Lilah rummages through the cabinet in her quest to find caffeine.

"Art and Josh got into a really bad fight. They beat the holy shit out of each other. It was awful."

"Damn. I wish I was there to see their fine asses fighting. I bet it was like watching porn."

"Lilah, will you get your head out of the fucking clouds? There was nothing sexy about blood spilling everywhere."

"I bet the blood made it hotter." She bites her bottom lip.

"You're sick."

"You saw the fight of a lifetime, and all you can do is complain!" Lilah exclaims.

"Make the damn coffee," I say, sitting at the small breakfast nook situated across from the refrigerator.

"So demanding."

After a few minutes, she sits beside me, handing me a mug of the delicious smelling brew.

I close my eyes, savoring the taste as I slowly sip the hot beverage.

"Is Art fucking anybody?"

I jerk, spilling coffee on my arm. "Shit."

"I'll get you some ice."

"How would I know who he's fucking?" I snatch the ice-filled Ziplock bag offered to me, pressing it to my reddening skin.

"You could've overheard him on the phone talking to a girl or something." She takes her seat again.

"Well, I haven't."

"Oh, okay. Bri and I were wondering why he hasn't taken us up on our offer for a threesome."

It takes Lilah awhile to get over a crush, but I was sure Bri—who has the attention span of a fly—would've moved on by now. They must really like him. If my secret comes to light, Trevor won't be the only one affected by my betrayal.

"So now you and Bri are okay with sharing?"

"I guess so. Fighting over Art wasn't getting us anywhere, so we decided on a temporary truce."

"It could be that he's not interested in either of you."

"A boy doesn't have to be interested in a girl to have sex."

"Is sex the only thing you want from him?"

"Of course not, silly. I plan to fuck him so good he'll be pussy whipped and want to be my boyfriend."

"Sex won't hold a guy's attention for long. Anyway, what about Bri? Doesn't she want Art to be her boyfriend too?"

"He'll choose me over her."

This conversation is giving me a headache.

"Don't be stupid. You and Bri have been throwing yourselves at him for the last few weeks like complete idiots. If he wanted to fuck, he would have by now. He obviously doesn't want either of you." I want to kick my own ass for causing the crestfallen expression on her face. "I'm sorry."

"You know, Cin, not everyone can have the perfect relationship with the boy next door. Trevor wants a future with you. You have an excellent GPA, and you're a track star with a full ride to an amazing school. You have a big, bright future. I envy you."

"You have a lot going for yourself."

"I'll be lucky if I graduate. I haven't applied to a single college."

"What?"

"I've been lying to my parents about that. College isn't for me, but they don't understand. I have no idea what I'm going to do." Tears spring to her eyes and spill down her cheeks.

I reach over and give her a one-arm hug. "We'll figure this out, together. You like hair, nails, and makeup, so there's cosmetology school. Community college is also an option."

She kisses my cheek. "What would I do without you?"

"This is a lovely sight to see first thing in the morning—cousins bonding over coffee." Katrina helps herself to the coffee before joining us at the breakfast nook.

She is almost the exact replica of my mom, only a little taller with thinner lips and wider eyes.

"Good morning," I say.

"Morning." Katrina takes a sip of her drink. "I'm cool, right?"

"Sure."

"Mom, if you have to ask, you're totally not cool."

"That's why you're my favorite niece," she says to me, completely ignoring Lilah's statement.

"I'm your only niece." I giggle.

"Since I'm such a cool adult can I be included in the girl talk?" Katrina waggles her eyebrows.

Lilah rolls her eyes. "What we were discussing is between us."

Katrina pokes out her bottom lip and gives me her saddest expression.

"Sorry, my lips are sealed." I move my fingers across my lips in a zipping motion.

"Fine." Her lips morph from a pout into a wide smile. Nothing keeps Katrina down for long.

"I'm excited you're here. We can talk about Missy's surprise party."

Though my mom's birthday is on Sunday, my aunt knows how to party hard and doesn't want to work on Monday with a hangover, so Saturday was the better option. There are four buildings on this plot of land. The main house, stable, vet clinic, and a guesthouse Katrina and Thomas had built a few years back. The guesthouse is where my friends and I used to party and have fun. Unfortunately our last get-together got out of control and Lilah's father forbade her from stepping inside again. He even changed the locks. That's where the surprise party will be.

"Missy thinks Ricky is taking her to some fancy restaurant for dinner on Saturday evening. He's going to blindfold her and drive around for about forty-five minutes. They should arrive by eight o'clock, so I need you girls to be ready by four o'clock to help me with decorations."

"You can count on me, Auntie."

"I guess I could help," Lilah mutters.

"Awesome!"

"What's on the menu?" I ask.

"Tons of good ole Southern dishes. The caterer and DJ are scheduled to arrive at six o'clock."

"Wow, you're going all out."

"Of course, it's a big day for Missy."

"Mom!" Dionte comes running into the room, distressed.

"What is it?"

"I can't find my Nintendo Switch, and I know Lilah took it." He throws her an accusatory look, pointing a finger at her.

"Lilah?"

"Did you see me take it?"

"I fell asleep with it on my bed."

"What did I tell you about staying up late playing games?" Katrina asks.

"Yeah, brat. Your brain cells are probably mush by now," Lilah says.

"Do you have his game or not?"

"I told him to stay out of my bedroom and out of my things."

"Give it back to him."

"I'm not giving the little booger a thing."

"Now," Katrina says sternly.

"Why is it he gets away with everything, but the moment I do something wrong, it's the end of the world? I hate it here!"

"That's not true," Katrina says.

"Yes, it is!" Lilah wails.

"Stay out of your sister's room." Katrina grasps Dionte's chin. "The next time you'll be punished for two weeks—no games, cell phone, or TV."

"But, Mom—"

"No buts. Do you understand?"

"Yes."

"Great, the matter is settled. Lilah, if you could be so kind as to give your brother back his game, I would really appreciate it."

Lilah leaves the kitchen with a satisfied look on her face, with Dionte following behind.

"Is it possible to love two boys at the same time?" I blurt.

I'm comfortable talking to Katrina about this topic. I know she'll give me sound advice and won't judge me. Unlike my mom, she won't assume the worst.

"Yes, that's absolutely possible. Do you love two boys?"

"I think so. I mean it feels like I do. What should I do?"

"I can't answer that question for you. Do what you feel is right, here." She touches my stomach. "Your gut instinct will help you through this. Your heart and brain aren't reliable. One is filled with emotions, while the other will overanalyze the situation."

"I'm so confused. I know with Trevor, there's a possibility we'll remain together through college and get married. He's safer. The other boy is an unknown variable, but the way he makes me feel... Trevor has never made me feel that way. I don't even know if this boy has even contemplated a future with me because he doesn't see one for himself."

"If you had to make the decision today to never see or talk to one of them again, who would you choose?"

"The thought of being without either of them makes me sick." Fuck. I was hoping she would say dump the other boy and stay with Trevor. I should've known she wouldn't make this decision easy for me. "Am I a horrible person?"

"No, sweetheart. You're young and allowed to make mistakes. Life is about trial and error, so trust me, you'll make plenty more."

"Some people would say I'm selfish and have no morals."

"And I say fuck them. 'Do not judge, lest ye be judged.' No one on this earth is so perfect they can judge anyone else. If you decide to be with Trevor, you'll have to tell him the truth. No secret can stay buried forever. He may forgive you, and the two of you can move on, or maybe he won't. You made the conscious choice to cheat, so you must face the consequences. This will be a life lesson for you. One you'll always remember."

"Thank you, Auntie." I give her a hug.
"You're welcome, Niecy."

CHAPTER twenty seven

ART

My eyes roam over her body. I can't help it. I look away when I realize what I'm doing, but it's nearly impossible to keep my gaze from wandering back to her. It doesn't help that she looks fucking good tonight, hanging up her baggy, unappealing clothes to wear a form-hugging gold dress. No heels—I doubt if my girl knows how to walk in those—but the black Chuck Taylors she paired with the dress works. She walks around, smiling and socializing with guests, with that asshole Trevor at her side. Damn if I don't wish it were me. Cin is supposed to be a convenient fuck, that's all, but she's becoming so much more.

The bottom line is she's not for me because she deserves so much better, not an ex-drug addict and suicide survivor who's responsible for the death of his little brother. I wouldn't be able to give her my all. Would she even leave Trevor for me? It's probably better not to rock the boat. I'll enjoy her while I can. We've been sating our uncontrolled lust by fucking almost every night like wild beasts. The cutting has stopped, but my nightmares continue to haunt me. Damn, she makes me want to be a better person.

"Hello, earth to Art. Is anyone home?"

I reluctantly pull my gaze from the girl I've become obsessed with. I'm not here to witness the joyous moment when Ricky proposes to Missy. Cin's the sole reason I decided to come.

"What?" I take a big gulp of sweet tea.

"You haven't been able to take your eyes off of her for the last hour."

"Who are you talking about?"

"Don't play dumb."

Lilah is fucking annoying. She's been hounding me like a dog chasing a bone ever since I arrived at the party. Whenever I move, so does she.

"If you have something to say, say it. I'm no good at guessing games."

"You like her."

"Who do I supposedly like?"

"Cin."

"What if I do? How is it any of your business?"

"Everyone else wants her, so why not you?" Lilah walks away.

What the hell is that comment supposed to mean?

Josh appears at my left. "Are you enjoying the party?"

"Why are you talking to me?"

"There's nothing wrong with engaging in small talk."

"Next we can start trimming each other's pubic hairs."

"Don't be a dick."

"I can't help it. It's my nature."

Ever since the fight, Josh and I have a newfound respect for each other—though Ricky nearly blew a gasket when he saw our faces later that day.

"Don't try to suck up to me because I beat your ass."

"You did not beat my ass. I laid you flat, and you know it." Josh snorts.

That he did. My back still hurts a little.

"If that lie is what helps you sleep at night…" I shrug a shoulder.

"Look, I wanted to say sorry for not staying behind the other night and taking the blame with you. I know it was a shitty move. Can we let bygones be bygones? What do you say?" He holds his hand out to me.

I look at it suspiciously, not entirely sure I should trust him.

"Don't leave me hanging, man."

I grasp his hand and give it a firm shake. "This does not mean I'm going to trim your pubic hairs."

He laughs. "You know you want to."

I grunt in response.

"What did you say to Lilah? She looks pissed."

"Nothing, she must be PMSing."

From the corner of my eye, I notice Cin leave the house. "Anyway, thanks for the girl talk, but I have to take a piss, unless you want to come with me."

"I'll pass."

"Damn and I was so looking forward to continuing this conversation."

It's time for me to catch my girl alone.

Cin

Art is making it really awkward to be in the same room with him. He's basically telling everyone here without words that he wants to spread my legs open and go berserk on my pussy. Trevor and I sit at one of the rectangular tables my aunt rented. The spacious living room has been transformed. Ricky and Thomas moved all the furniture into a storage shed. The expression of happiness on my mom's face was priceless when the blindfold was removed and everyone yelled surprise. She will always remember her thirty-eighth birthday.

"I swear if this wasn't your mom's party, I would knock his eyeballs right out of his head."

"It's not a big deal."

"Yes, it fucking is. He's always watching you, like you're a big, juicy steak." Trevor pops a fried catfish nugget into his mouth.

"In a few more months, we'll never see him again." Those words cause a pinging sensation in my chest.

"Has he ever tried to fuck you?"

"No. Don't be stupid." I'm surprised I don't look like Pinocchio by now.

"Don't lie to me."

"He hasn't."

He stares at me so long I think he's going to press the issue. "I'm going to get some more food. Do you want anything?"

"No."

Firstly, even if I wanted to end it with Art, he wouldn't let me. Secondly, avoiding him would be impossible since we live in the same house. Lastly, I know this makes me lower than dirt, but I'm not ready to end it with him. I want them both.

"Have you seen Lilah?" Katrina asks as she walks towards me.

"Not for some time. Do you need help with something?"

"Can you be a darling and grab your mother's birthday gift from the main house for me?"

"Sure. Where is it?"

"I left it on top of the dresser in my bedroom. You can't miss it."

"I'll be back in a few minutes."

"Thanks."

"No problem."

I could use a bit of fresh air and a reprieve from Art's piercing gaze, so I gladly leave the guesthouse. When I step through the front door of the main house, hands latch onto my breasts from behind and warm lips brush along my neck. The door is slammed shut.

"Art," I moan.

"The moment I saw you in this dress, I wanted to bend you over and fuck the shit out of you," he whispers in my ear.

One hand leaves my breast to seize my hair, positioning my head to receive his plundering tongue. His other hand ventures between my legs to grip my heat through the dress. He steers me towards the sofa where he bends me over the back. My pussy quivers in anticipation when he lifts the dress over my ass and tugs my panties to my knees. His belt buckle slaps against my bottom as he undoes his pants.

I squeeze the soft cushions of the sofa, my eyes fluttering close when the thick mushroom head of his dick opens my hungry cunt. In and out, he works his massive length until he impales me completely. All thought leaves my mind when he goes postal on my pussy, rapidly delivering powerful strokes with enough force to move the sofa up the carpet. With each thrust forward, he jerks my hips back to meet his punishing blows. I tether on the edge of oblivion before finally falling into ecstasy. My limbs turn to liquid and I slide to the floor. Art follows, his hardness still buried in my pussy. His muscular chest molds to my back, pushing my body into the plush carpet as he continues the relentless assault. Art shouts, reaching his climax.

"Sinking inside you makes me believe in heaven on earth." He kisses my ear.

"*Eu te amo*." I bite my tongue.

"What did you say?"

"Nothing."

"I fucking knew it." Lilah stands in the doorway with a murderous expression on her face.

Shit, it's all over. What the hell was I thinking having sex with Art in the middle of my aunt's living room?

"Slut," she sneers.

Art pushes to his feet, putting his dick back in his pants, then helps me up.

"Why stop at one cousin, when you can have them both?"

Whatever Art was expecting, it sure as hell wasn't what Lilah just said. His expression turns thunderous.

"What the fuck is she talking about?"

"Oh, she didn't tell you about her and Josh?"

"Lilah, don't."

"Tell me," Art demands.

"They hooked up."

"Is that true?"

"I can explain."

"You can fucking explain?" he booms, startling me.

"Art—"

"Did you fuck the rest of the gang too?"

"Fucking bastard," I say.

"I can't believe you did this, Cin," Lilah says, turning to leave.

"Lilah, wait! Please don't tell Trevor!"

"Fuck you, bitch."

Art jerks away when I make a grab for him as he moves past me. His hand latches onto my throat, crushing my windpipe.

"Keep your goddamn hands off me. No wonder you gave it to me so easily. You probably spread your legs for every boy who wants to fuck."

He flings me back and I hit the floor, landing on my wrist. By the time I recover and make it outside, Art is already traveling down the road on his motorcycle. I clutch my throbbing wrist to my stomach, racing to the guesthouse, fearing Lilah already exposed my secret to Trevor.

"Cin, where have you been? Ricky is about to propose," Katrina asks.

"Have you seen Lilah and Trevor?"

"They're around here somewhere." She looks at my hands. "Where's the gift?"

"I'm sorry. I didn't see it."

"Are you okay?"

"Yeah, I'm fine."

"You don't seem fine."

The music goes silent.

"Can I have everyone's attention, please?" Ricky announces.

Katrina squeals in delight. "It's about to happen."

"I want to thank all of you for helping me make the special lady in my life's birthday celebration a success." Ricky grabs my mom's hand. "Having you by my side for the last few years has added value to my life. I want you with me, always." He gets down on one knee.

The room erupts in excited shouts. She covers her mouth and tears start flowing from her eyes. The joyous moment is clouded by the shitstorm on the horizon. I look to the left, spotting Lilah and Trevor talking.

Oh my God.

Trevor's eyes connect with mine, causing my heart to thunder in my chest. It feels like I'm about to hurl as he approaches, studying my face intently.

"What's the matter?"

"What were you talking about with Lilah?"

"The party, this is awesome."

She didn't tell him. Maybe her plan is to blackmail me. "Congratulations" resound through the room. Damn, I missed the end of the proposal. Ricky and my mom hold each other in a tight embrace.

"Yeah, she did an amazing job."

"You look pale and you're sweating."

"I'm not feeling like myself. I'm going to go home and get some rest."

"I'll drive you."

"No, I have to get my car home."

"You shouldn't be driving. I'll make sure it's dropped off later."

"I'm okay. I just need to lie down for a bit."

"I can't let you—"

"I'm going to be fine. I want you to stay and have a good time."

"All right, Ms. Independent, but only on one condition."

I nod.

"Text me when you get home."

"Deal."

"I'll walk you to your car."

"I'm not a baby. Trust me, I can manage."

"Fine, I'll check on you tomorrow." He gives me a peck on the lips.

"Tell my mom I wasn't feeling well if she asks about me. With all the excitement, she probably won't notice I'm gone."

"Sure thing, babe."

I move towards the door on fast feet, but Lilah steps in my path.

"Leaving so soon?"

"Why didn't you tell?"

"You'll fall flat on your face soon enough, and I'll be there to watch the aftermath."

"I didn't mean for this to happen."

"Spare me the 'it was a mistake' bullshit. How long have you been cheating on Trevor? I know this isn't the first time. Art loves you. I saw it in the way he watched you tonight."

Could there be some truth to what she's saying? Does Art love me?

"You have no idea what Art is going through. I just wanted to help him."

"By fucking him? How is that working out?"

There's nothing I can say to defend my actions.

"You knew I liked him this whole time. I must have been a joke to both of you."

"No, that's not true. I never intended to hurt you. I'm so sorry."

"I'm so tired of everyone praising you. The perfect daughter and the fucking perfect niece. I was so happy when you moved here, but soon enough I wished you gone."

"So, this is how you really feel about me?"

"I've liked Trevor since junior high school and just when he started noticing me, you came along."

"That's not fair. You never told me you had a thing for him."

"Would it have mattered?"

"Yes."

"It didn't matter to you about Art. Anyway, I didn't want to seem like a pathetic, needy bitch."

"Let's go back to the house and talk."

"No. Home will never be the same, not after what I witnessed in the living room. At least now I know why Art never gave Bri or me the time of day."

"I…" I have no idea what to say.

"You have two boys who love you, when I've never had one."

"We can get past this. We'll always be cousins."

"Not by choice." She walks away.

I was surprised to see Art's motorcycle parked outside when I got home. I thought in his anger, he would spend a few hours riding to calm down. I stayed in the car for a good twenty minutes before I worked up the nerve to go inside.

"Art," I call through his door.

"If you know what's good for you, you would get the hell away from my door and stay away from me. If you don't, I swear to God, I'll hurt you."

"I just want to explain."

A loud bang sounds at the door. "Leave!"

"I'm not leaving until you talk to me."

A furious Art swings the door open. His heaving chest is covered in blood from new cuts.

"What did you do to yourself?"

I scream when he throws me into the wall and grasps my jaw in a painful hold. His nails pierce my skin. His eyes are wild, and foam drips from his mouth. For the first time, I'm actually afraid of him. I should've left well enough alone, given him a few days to get his temper under control.

"You just don't know when to fucking quit."

"Listen—"

"I'm not interested in anything you have to say!"

I whimper when his hold gets tighter.

"From now on, you're going to stay the fuck away from me. When you see me coming, turn the other way. This is the only warning I'm going to give you."

He releases me, then goes back into his bedroom, slamming the door shut. I run my fingers along the torn flesh of my jaw, smearing blood on them. The truth isn't as bad as it seems, but he won't listen. I lock myself in my bedroom for the remainder of the night. This is probably for the best. I knew it would come to an end eventually.

Cin

The last week and a half has been a nightmare. The tension at home and school is making me a nervous wreck. I've been staying in my bedroom for the most part, and if I happen upon Art alone, I quickly turn the other way. Art stays in his bedroom too, even refusing to come out to dinner, but it's impossible to completely avoid the people you live with. Ricky had to intervene on several occasions to prevent Art and Josh from fighting. Everyone is curious about what caused the rift between Lilah and me, but I've kept my mouth shut. Lilah and Art have done the same. I can understand her reasoning, but I can't fathom why he hasn't let the cat out of the bag. Maybe, like Lilah, he's waiting for me to fall flat on my face.

It's hard to concentrate in first period. I'm afraid Art will suddenly change his mind about not talking, but he sits at his desk, not sparing Trevor or me a glance. He ignores me in trigonometry too. I wish he would let me explain, but I haven't tried to talk to him since that night because, frankly, he scared the shit out of me. Even Bri gave up on him after he told her to fuck off in the hall last week for all present to hear. The severe hit to her ego won't allow her to seek him again. My eyes steadily roam towards the classroom door, but Art never comes to first period. I don't know whether to be happy or concerned. Later, I spot him talking to Bane while I was walking to the cafeteria with Anneli. Why is he talking to him?

"Are you going to tell me what's going on?"

"I already told you, nothing."

"And the sky is green," Anneli says.

"Really? I thought it was yellow."

"Don't lie to me, Cin. It must be pretty bad since Lilah stopped coming to sit with us at lunch."

"I'm not in the mood to talk about this."

"We're best friends. I thought you trusted me."

"I do."

"Does it have anything to do with Art?"

"You mean a lot to me. I couldn't ask for a better person in my corner, but I'm not ready to tell you about everything I've done."

"Okay. No pressure. Whenever you're ready to talk, I'll be here."

She'll help me pick up the pieces when I find the courage to tell her everything. Anneli and I grab two slices of cheese pizza each before heading to the table. I glance around the large space, looking for Art.

"I cannot wait until the school year is over so I can be free of him," Josh says.

"You said after the fight, you two had an understanding. What changed?" Dex pops a few fries in his mouth.

"I thought so too. I'm really trying not to be an ass to him today, especially since it's his brother's birthday."

"You should've said something sooner," I say.

"Why?"

"Use your brain, for God's sake. He shouldn't be alone today." Anneli rolls her eyes.

"He didn't come to class this morning," Trevor says.

Josh pales a little. "He's home alone since Missy and my dad are making deliveries today. You don't think he would…"

"I saw him in the hall a few minutes ago," I say to assure everyone. "He probably needed a little time to get himself together this morning, that's all."

My heart is telling me to seek him out and offer comfort, but my mind knows he'll reject support from me. I'll try to talk to him in class this afternoon, his reaction be damned. I can't let him hurt alone.

It's been almost twenty-five minutes since trigonometry class started, but still Art hasn't arrived. I can't shake the feeling that something is terribly wrong. Did he go back home? Why did he come to school just to talk to Bane?

I raise my hand.

"Yes?"

"Can I go to the bathroom?"

"Come get the hall pass."

I head straight for Bane's hideout spot. He's notorious for cutting class. I enter the vacant classroom on the ground level. Bane sits on a desk, watching his friends shoot dice. Beer bottles litter the floor. I don't understand why they come to school at all.

"Looky what we have here." Jesse stands from his crouched position. "Not my usual type. Too damn skinny, but I'll make an exception."

"Back off, you know that's Trevor's girl." Bane puffs on his cigarette. "I don't need to be on his shit list."

"I'm not afraid of her pussy-ass boyfriend or stepbrother." He twirls my hair around his finger.

I elbow him in the stomach. "You can look, but no touching."

His friends laugh.

"Burn, Jesse," I hear one of them say.

"Fucking bitch," he snarls, clasping my arm.

"I told you to leave her alone."

Jesse looks me up and down, then resumes the game with his friends.

"What do you want? I didn't think you would be the type to ever seek me out."

"I saw you talking to Art earlier."

"The last time I checked, the US of A is a free country, giving me the right to talk to whomever the fuck I want."

"What did he want?"

"What kind of supplier would I be if I went around breaching customer confidentiality?"

"Did you sell him drugs?" Art should never have been left alone today.

"You're sticking your nose where it doesn't belong. It's time for you to leave," Bane says.

"You don't realize what you've done." I race from the classroom.

Art has to be stopped before it's too late. I run towards the nearest exit as fast as my feet will carry me and hop in my car. Pressing down on the gas pedal, I speed out of the parking lot.

Racing inside the house, I make a beeline for Art's bedroom. I don't want to alert him to my arrival, so I'm sure to keep quiet, but he's not there. Next, I go to the dining room and that's where I find Art, sitting at the table with a few lines of cocaine before him. He has a bill rolled in the shape of a straw, preparing to snort the addictive drug.

"Art, no!" I shout, sweeping my hand across the table to scatter the powder onto the floor.

"Bitch!" He hops from the chair, pushing me to the floor. "What have you done?"

"I can't let you go down that dark path again. I know it's your brother's birthday, but there are other ways to cope. Let me help you." I plead with him to understand.

"Fuck! I needed that!" He rakes his hands through his hair. "You're fucking dead."

Sensing I'm in mortal danger, self-preservation takes over and I jump to my feet. Art chases me around the table. I stop when he does and watch him from the other side.

"By tomorrow morning, you would've hated yourself if I hadn't stopped you."

"I already hate myself." He leaps onto the table.

Screaming, I swiftly turn on my heel and barrel through the door leading to the kitchen. I don't make it far before Art grabs my hair, wrenching me back. I twist around and sink my teeth into his arm, then break away when his hold loosens. I run through the house, afraid to take the time to unlock the front door to make good on my escape with Art only steps behind. He grabs my left ankle as I take two stairs at a time, causing me to fall with a jolt. Fight replaces flight, and I kick out my right leg, hitting him in the face. Though he stumbles a little, he recovers within seconds, the kick having little effect on him. Still, I'm given a slight advantage. It's all I need to make it safely to my bedroom where I can lock the door and hide out until someone comes home. I make it to my safe haven, swinging the door forward, but it's too late. Art stops the door from closing, flinging it back open with enough force that I'm struck in the face. I fall to the floor, shouting out in pain.

Before I can decide on my next move, Art throws his heavy body on top of mine, pinning my wrists above my head and preventing further action.

"Think about what you're about to do. You really don't want to hurt me." I struggle beneath him.

I'm not sure what he's really capable of. I'm alone with an unstable boy, and the nearest neighbor is a mile down the road. No one will hear my cries for help.

"You want more of my dick? Is that it? I'm sorry. You'll have to get your appetite sated by Trevor or Josh from now on." He bares his teeth.

"Josh and I never had sex."

"Stop lying!"

"It's true! You have it all wrong."

"That's not what Lilah said."

"I didn't kiss Josh. He kissed me, but that's it. I promise you, Art."

"Why should I believe you when you're cheating on Trevor with me? You don't understand the word faithful."

"How can you judge me? So, it's okay if I cheat on Trevor, but only with you?"

"Yes!" He attacks my lips ruthlessly.

I return his kiss with a ferociousness of my own, drunk off the onslaught of his lust. Art rises to his knees, tugging down my sweatpants. I grasp his hands, stopping him.

"No, I'm on my period."

"Blood doesn't scare me. I need you now." He pulls my bottoms and panties off.

Even if I wanted to, I couldn't deny him, not when my desire for him surpasses any emotion I've ever experienced in my young life. I spread my legs, eagerly waiting for him to fuck me. He frees his beautiful dick, which juts from a nest of fine black curls. Having sex while on my period will be the most taboo thing I've ever done. He pulls the tampon from my center, tossing the blood-soaked cotton to the floor. The intimacy of this moment will be burned in my memories forever. He guides my legs over his shoulders before driving into my opening. My pussy curves to his dick perfectly, almost as if I were created for him.

He fucks me aggressively, showing me no mercy, and I love every fucking second of it. We cling to each other, both new to the exquisite passion we share.

"I thought I'd already hit rock bottom, but you came along and introduced me to a new hell. You'll be my destruction."

"I don't want to destroy you."

"I nearly lost my fucking mind without talking to you, touching you, breathing you…" He groans.

Violent tremors rack my entire body, momentarily rendering me unable to form words. Art's shout of pleasure rings through my ears. Afterwards, we shower together then scrub the blood from the carpet. I never imagined period sex could be so damn amazing.

CHAPTER twenty nine

Cin

The next day, I devise a plan to help Art find closure. I'll need his full cooperation for it to be successful. This weekend is the perfect opportunity, since Josh and Trevor are going on a fishing trip with Ricky. Ricky insisted Art join them, but not surprisingly, he vehemently refused. My mom and aunt, along with some of their friends, will be traveling to Las Vegas for a girls' getaway Friday morning. They think I'll be staying with Anneli. It was like pulling teeth to persuade her to cover for me, but she relented after I explained my reasoning. Once I'm sure everyone has left Saturday morning, I drive home before the sun brightens the dark sky.

I find Art awake, lying on his bed. "Get dressed. We're going on a road trip."

He glances up from his cell phone. "Is that right?"

"Yep."

"Where are we going?"

"Boston."

"Why?"

"We're going to visit Cole's grave."

"I'm not going there."

"You need—"

"Drop it."

"No."

"Excuse me?"

"No, I will not drop it. We're going."

"I'm not having this conversation."

"I'm not leaving this room until you do."

"It would take me no effort to pick your little ass up and throw you out."

"Fucking pussy."

"I hate to break it to you, but reverse psychology doesn't work on me."

"You owe it to your brother to go."

"Watch it. You're treading on dangerous ground."

"If it'll get you to go, I'll stomp all over the motherfucker."

"Get out."

"I'm not going anywhere."

Art tosses his cell phone on the bed before standing. The dangerous ground he spoke of is about to crack, but I refuse to back down. He stops directly in front of me, stooping to my level until our eyelashes kiss.

"Don't make me fuck you up," he threatens.

"Stop acting like a pansy-ass punk!"

He clutches my shoulders and shakes me so violently, I begin to feel dizzy as my teeth clank together.

"I swear to God, I'll break your fucking fingers."

"Will that make you feel better?" I shout.

"Yes!" he snarls.

"Show Cole you love him. Show him you haven't forgotten about him." I caress his face.

"I can't," he chokes.

"I know everything inside you is rebelling against taking this leap, but Art, you need to do this."

He remains silent for a few minutes before speaking, but still it's a small victory for me.

"I'll go, but I want something in return."

I should've known there would be a catch. "Name it."

"No, I'm not going to tell you, but when the time comes for you to pay your debt, no questions asked."

"How can I agree when you won't tell me what the condition is?"

"Take it or leave it."

"I'll take it."

It really doesn't matter what he wants, I guess. I'd do anything to get him to go.

"I have to buy you a helmet."

"That won't be necessary."

"Yes, it is. I'll risk my life, but not yours."

"It's not necessary because I'm not getting on that death trap. We can take my car."

"That old piece of crap won't make it past Pennsylvania."

"Hey, respect the car. It may be old, but it's very reliable."

"Okay, but it'll be your fault it we end up stuck on the side of the road."

ART

Maybe I shouldn't have let Cin talk me into doing this. I descend further into panic-attack mode the closer we get to Boston.

Suck it the fuck up, pussy.

This visit is long overdue.

"Why are you so quiet? You've barely spoken two words since you got into the car."

I turn my gaze from the scenery I've watched for the last several hours to peer at Cin. "Just thinking."

"You're scared."

"Shitless." When did it become so easy for me to admit my vulnerabilities to her?

"I'm surprised you gave in."

"So am I."

"Why did you?"

"It's time to face my demons."

"You don't have to face them alone. I'll be there to support you every step of the way. If you want me to wait in the car, I can do that, or if you want me to walk with you to Cole's gravesite, I can do that too. Whatever you need."

I'm falling in love with this girl. I don't deserve her or happiness. Walking away from her will be one of the hardest things I'll ever do. I hate to admit it, but Trevor isn't so bad. He'll treat Cin right, and that's what matters.

"Thank you." I can't remember the last time I made that statement and meant it.

"You're welcome."

I become lost in the beautiful smile she rewards me with.

"You hungry?"

I clear my throat. "I could eat."

"According to the GPS, we're in Hagerstown, Maryland. Ever stop here?"

"No, only drove through."

"Check to see what restaurants are around."

"What are you in the mood for?"
"I could use a big, fat, juicy burger."
"Got it." I do a quick search. "What about Dixie's Burger Joint?"
"Sounds good."

Cin

"Are you planning on visiting your parents while we're in Boston?" I take a bite of my burger.

"Nope."

"Do you think you'll ever forgive them?"

"They don't deserve forgiveness."

"What about your grandfather? What has he done to make you hate him so much?"

"He's a manipulative, narcissistic prick." Art laughs. "And I'm just like him."

"You're not."

Why can't Art see he's so much more than what he believes?

"I won't deny who I am. I'm not the hero, Cin. I'm the antihero. There's no goodness in me, so don't look for it because you'll be disappointed."

"You're your own worst enemy."

"Why does it matter, anyway? In several months, we'll never see each other again. After college, you'll marry your high school sweetheart, then pop out a few brats."

He might as well have thrown a glass of cold water in my face like the night we first met. I can't stomach the thought of never seeing him again. I'll always wonder if he's hurting, using cocaine again, or worse.

"Your uncle is marrying my mom, so we'll see each other again."

"I'm not going to the wedding. I'll be a legal adult way before then, doing whatever the hell I want, with no one getting in my way."

"You can visit for Thanksgiving, Christmas, and other holidays." I'm grasping at straws, and I know it.

"Do you think I'm going to carve the turkey while Trevor holds the fork in it? Wake the fuck up. While everyone's watching football, are we going to sneak to the bathroom for a quickie? You're living in a dreamland."

I drop the burger on the plate, suddenly losing my appetite.

"Are you done?"

I nod.

"Good, let's go."

ART

"Can I ask you something?"

Now what? My hands clench the steering wheel, turning my knuckles white. "You said you were tired, so go to sleep."

"How old were you when you started using cocaine?"

"Thirteen."

"How does a thirteen-year-old get introduced to a drug like that?"

"One of my mother's associates."

"You're shitting me."

"I shit you not."

"That's child abuse!" Cin says in outrage. "Does your mom know?"

"Nah. She introduced me to sex too."

"The bitch is a pedophile? Art, you should've told someone. You still could."

"I liked every minute of it."

"Duh, at thirteen, I'm sure your hormones were running wild. But she took advantage of you."

"What's done is done."

"When did it stop?"

"We continued to fuck until Cole's death."

"You haven't seen her since?"

"I've seen her."

"Did you fuck her?"

"No."

"Why?"

"I wasn't interested in having sex with anyone at that time."

"She should be in jail."

"You should be thanking her."

"Are you mad?" Cin sputters.

"How do you think I learned to fuck the way I do? Not many teenage boys fuck like me. I've made you orgasm in less than three minutes more than once by eating your pussy. I bet Trevor has never done that."

"If I had to choose between you not being molested or me being fucked well, I'd choose the former."

"How old were you when you lost your virginity?"

"Sixteen."

"With Trevor?"

"Yes."

"He's the only one you've been with besides me?"

"Yes. How many girls have you been with?"

"Shit if I know."

"Have you ever had a girlfriend?"

"Nope."

"Why?"

"Having one never appealed to me."

The entrance to the cemetery appears in the distance. How the hell did we get here so fast?

"We're here," I croak.

"Do you remember where he's buried?"

"I could never forget."

I drive through the gates and park near the cedar tree where Cole rests.

I lay my head against the steering wheel, hyperventilating.

"I. Can't. Breathe."

Cin rubs my back with a firm, reassuring hand. "It's okay. We can stay in the car for a little while."

Get yourself together, Art. You didn't come all this way to not follow through.

I compose myself. "No, I'm ready."

"Are you sure?"

"Hell no." I open the car door and step out on shaky legs.

My stomach feels like it's filled with butterflies. I break out in a cold sweat before I hunch over and vomit. Again, Cin offers me unwavering support, running to my side. I heave until there's nothing left, then drop to the ground, hanging my head between my drawn-up knees. Cin grasps my face and lifts my head to place a soft kiss on my lips. She stands, offering me her hand. I should've known from the moment she threw her glass of water in my face that she would destroy the carefully constructed wall I built around myself. What would I be doing right this very second had I not been shipped off to North Carolina? How different would things have been had I never been introduced to a life of Cin? I slide my hand into her much smaller one before slowly pushing up from the ground. We walk towards the cedar tree. My steps falter when the top of Cole's gravestone comes into my line of vision.

"We're almost there." She squeezes my hand.

A photo of Cole is engraved in granite with an angel sitting on each side of the black rock. I fall to my knees, tracing the words *In Loving Memory of Cole King*. I shout, loud and long—all the pent-up rage, guilt, hate, and grief spilling from the depths of my soul. I wouldn't wish this pain on anyone.

"Why?" I scream, tilting my head to the sky.

Cin kneels on the grass beside me, a lifeline in my fucked-up universe.

"Cole, I didn't mean for this to happen. I'm so sorry I wasn't there for you. I'm so sorry I wasn't the big brother you needed me to be. I love you so much." Tears spill from my eyes.

"He knows you love him." Cin kisses my cheek.

I brush my thumb across her wet face. "You're crying for me."

"Your pain is my pain."

"I want to hold him in my arms one more time."

"I know. You can't see or physically touch him, but he'll always be with you."

"You've given me something I never thought I'd have again."

"What?"

"Hope."

"I'll be right back."

I watch Cin as she walks to the car and retrieves a bag, before coming back to sit at my hip.

"I thought it would be good to give Cole a small gift for his birthday." She reaches into her bag, pulling out a Hulk action figure to place in front of the gravestone. "And I know he would enjoy hearing his big brother read a book about cars."

"Cin…" *I love you.*

She's peers at me expectantly.

"Thank you."

"You're welcome."

I take the book, opening it. There I sit and read, feeling a sense of peace for the first time since I found Cole's lifeless body floating in the pool.

CHAPTER thirty one

Cin

Art pulls into the parking lot of a tattoo shop a few hours later.

"What are we doing here?"

"You have a debt to pay."

"And what exactly do you have in mind?" I ask nervously.

"You're getting a tattoo."

"No, the hell I'm not!" I exclaim.

"You gave your word. There's no backing out now."

"A tattoo is so permanent."

"It doesn't matter. You agreed."

"Choose something else, anything."

"Nope, let's go."

"Art—"

He's out of the car, cutting off my protest. What the hell did I agree to? I enter the shop, finding Art at the counter. I come to a stop next to him.

"She's getting the tattoo."

The big burly man gives me a once-over.

"I need to see some ID," he says.

Thank God. Maybe there's a chance I could still get out of this, at least for the time being. Art retrieves a hundred-dollar bill from his wallet, sliding it over the counter.

"She lost her ID."

The man pushes the money back across the counter. "That's too bad."

Art tosses two more hundred-dollar bills on the counter. "Are you sure you can't make an exception?"

The man eyes the money, practically salivating at the mouth. Money may not be able to buy happiness, but it can buy a whole lot of other shit.

"This stays between us."

"Absolutely."

"What will you be getting today, little lady?"

"I…"

"It's a surprise," Art says.

"I have no say?"

"No, I choose."

"Bishop," the man yells.

"What?"

"Customers."

"This is my body."

"Trust me."

Reluctantly, I nod.

Once Bishop appears, he and Art have a private conversation. After my fate is sealed, we follow him to his station.

"Take off your shirt," Bishop directs me.

I peer over at Art who now sits on a stool. He mouths the word *trust*. I lift my top over my head, then throw it to Art.

"Sit in the chair backwards and pull down your left bra strap," Bishop says.

Of course I've thought about getting a tattoo before, but I wanted something with significant meaning. I'm not sure if I ever would've followed through. There's a lot of shit I wouldn't have done had I not met Art, but my heart rebels against the idea of never knowing him.

"Done," Bishop announces forty-five minutes later.

Art moves behind me to examine my new ink. "It's beautiful, just like I imagined. You ready to take a look?"

I take a deep breath. "Yes."

Art snaps a picture with his cell phone then shows me the image. A small majestic bird flies from an open birdcage on my upper left shoulder.

"It's amazing. Why did you choose this?"

"I was a bird locked in a cage until you set me free."

I'm unsure how to respond to that revelation.

"Come on. We have to get some rest before we hit the road."

"Okay," I say.

I leave the shop a confused mess.

ART

"I take it we're not going to stay at one of your family's hotels."

"I hadn't planned on it."

"Isn't staying at another hotel a conflict of interest?"

"We're not staying at a hotel."

"I'm not sleeping in the car."

I chuckle. "I don't expect you to."

"Well, where are we going to sleep?"

"I'm taking you to my house, and sleep will be the last thing on my mind." I plan on being inside her tight pussy for most of the night.

"I thought you said you didn't want to see your mom."

"I highly doubt she'll be home."

"What will you do if she is?"

"I didn't think that far ahead. We're here."

I maneuver the car right and type in the code at the gate before continuing on. Instead of heading for the garage I choose to park in the driveway.

"Wow, this house is humongous."

I attempt to view the brick-and-mortar house from Cin's perspective. I don't see what she does. My previous residence was similar to a mini-mall, much bigger than this. I take a lot of things for granted since living in a lap of luxury is nothing new to me, never wanting for anything except for better parents. Too bad money can't buy what I really need.

"The lights are on."

"That doesn't mean she's home. The lights are mostly kept on, and we also have a housekeeper."

I grab Cin's overnight bag from the back seat. Since most of my clothes are still here, I didn't bother packing anything. I unlock the front door, ushering Cin in first.

"Darling, I've missed you!" My mother walks from the back of the house with a gleeful expression, enveloping me in an unyielding embrace.

Just my fucking luck.

She must be on her way out since she's all dressed up. I clasp her arms, prying her from around my body.

"I'm so happy you're here." She peers at Cin. "And who is this?"

"Hi, I'm—"

I put the brakes on Cin's introduction. "None of your business."

"I've been waiting to hear back from you. I called, texted, left voicemails and messages with Ricky."

"So?"

"At least you're here now. You don't know how happy I am you came to visit me."

"I didn't."

Her smile vanishes. "Why did you come?"

"I owed Cole a visit."

"That's a huge milestone for you."

"Have fun on your date." I step around her.

"Let's have breakfast in the morning."

"We're leaving in a few hours."

"How about dinner? I'll cancel my plans."

"We ate already."

"Please, Art, I only want to talk."

"Can't, I'll be too busy fucking."

"Art!" Cin scolds.

I walk towards my bedroom with an angry Cin in tow. She starts in on me the moment I close the door.

"How can you treat your mother that way?"

"Easy."

"Give her a chance to redeem herself. She's hurting just as much as you."

"I don't need this shit from you!" I shout.

"You need to hear this!" she shouts back. "How would you feel if your mother died tomorrow?"

"Like I was on top of the world."

"You can't mean that."

"I mean every fucking word."

"You're not the heartless monster you have everyone believing you are."

"Get the fuck out. There's an empty room down the hall—sleep there."

"I'm not going anywhere."

"I'll throw you out on your fucking head."

"I'll fight if you do."

I pick Cin up and fling her over my shoulder. She kicks wildly while punching me. I drop her when sharp teeth chomp down on my lower back.

"You goddamn carnivore. If you want to eat something, eat my dick."

She clambers to her feet. "Bastard."

"I want to fuck you."

"I want you to fuck me."

We rip at each other's clothes, needing to feel the ultimate pleasure only we can create together. I slide my arms under Cin's knees, hoisting her up and pinning her against the wall. She pulls her tampon out, dropping it to the floor, then positions my erection at her wet opening. I thrust forward, fucking her with everything I have in me. A nuclear hit couldn't stop me. Our noses kiss when I press my sweat-covered forehead against hers. What Cin and I share is on another level of awareness, greater than physical contact. Sex provides temporary gratification, but what she gives me is so much more. The beast fell in love with the princess.

"Eu te amo," I whisper.

"You understood me."

"I speak several languages."

"Eu também te amo."

We come together, our bodies in perfect sync with one another. My life consists of two things now—*before* Cin and *after* Cin.

Cin

"You've been a bundle of excitement all day." I glance at Trevor from across the table.

We're at a new seafood restaurant that just opened a few counties over. Since it's Valentine's Day, Trevor insisted we go.

"Well, it's a special day."

"You know this day isn't a big deal for me." I take a bite of my crab cake sandwich.

"This one is."

"Why is that?"

"I got in."

"Got in what?"

"Lexington University! I haven't gotten the official acceptance letter in the mail yet, but I received an email a couple of days ago. I waited until today to tell you, as a bonus to your Valentine's Day gift."

"That's amazing."

Trevor will surely regret enrolling in the same college as me once he learns I've been unfaithful to him.

"Are you okay?"

"Yeah."

"I thought you'd be more thrilled."

"I am."

"You could show a little bit more excitement." He chuckles.

"I'm sorry. The coach was a drill sergeant at practice today, so I'm a bit tired."

"I have just the thing to cheer you up." He pulls a black box from his pocket.

The box contains a rectangular locket with our first initials inscribed on it.

"Open it."

Inside is a picture of us, smiling at the camera. We're so fucking happy. I can't stave off my tears.

"Babe, don't cry."

"It's so beautiful."

"I'm glad you like it."

I'm such a piece of shit, and what really makes me the scum of the earth is that if I had the power to undo it all, I wouldn't. I can't imagine not being with Art, not helping him. His demons would still be beating at him day and night if I hadn't pushed him the way I did. I led him out of a dark place. He still hasn't fully healed, and probably never will, but he's made a lot of progress.

"I love you so much, Cin. I want to make you happy."

More tears pour from my eyes at his proclamation. I've fallen into a routine, fucking both boys regularly, sometimes in the same night. I've dug myself in a hole, and as the days pass, the hole gets deeper and deeper. Soon, I won't be able to climb out. Each morning I tell myself this is the day I'll put my foot down with Art and tell Trevor everything, but I chicken out every single time. I don't want to hurt either of them. We'll be nursing our wounds for a long time after the storm clears.

Instead of going inside when Trevor takes me home, I get in my car and drive to Lilah's house. I'm not ready to go home yet. Anyway, a talk between us is long overdue. Thomas answers the door.

"Hi, Cin, how are you?"

"I'm good. How's the local Dr. Doolittle?"

"Super." He chuckles. "Lilah's in her bedroom."

"Thanks."

I don't bother knocking on her bedroom door. If she knows it's me, she'll probably lock it.

"What the fuck are you doing here?" Lilah looks up from polishing her toenails.

"We need to talk." I close the door.

"I have nothing to say to you."

I kick off my shoes, then sit cross-legged on her bed. "I have plenty to say to you."

"Save it."

"I'm sorry I hurt you."

"You knew it would hurt me before you did it."

"I know, and it's killing me," I cry.

"Then why aren't you dead yet?"

"There are things about Art you don't know."

"What makes you an expert on him? We've both only known Art for about two months now."

"Trust me. There are things you don't know."

"I'm all ears."

"I can't tell you."

"Why? I'm your cousin."

"I can't betray his trust."

"But you so easily betrayed Trevor's."

"The guilt is making me sick," I cry. "I love them both."

"Tell someone who gives a fuck."

"I'm not asking for your sympathy. I'm asking you to understand."

"Well, I don't."

"If it makes a difference, I'm breaking up with Trevor and staying away from Art."

"He lives in the same house as you," she scoffs.

"I'll be staying with Anneli most nights, and I was hoping I could crash here sometimes."

"That's a big fat no."

"You don't make apologizing easy."

"What's so special about you? Why do all the boys like you?"

"All the boys don't like me."

"The ones that count do." Lilah wipes a stray tear from her cheek.

"I never knew you had a crush on Trevor."

"Would it have mattered if you did?"

"Yes."

"But it didn't matter with Art."

"It's different with him."

"Right."

"I'm not perfect and never claimed to be, but neither are you."

"Don't turn this around on me."

"You only wanted Art for the thrill and nothing more. You don't give a shit about him. Your pride was bruised when he rejected you. That's the only reason you're mad. Be honest with yourself."

"Damn you."

I hit a nerve.

"I love you. I hope you'll forgive me one day." I leave the bed.

"Wait. Will you help me polish my nails?"

"Absolutely." I take the olive branch she offers.

"I'm still mad at you, but I guess it's not your fault you're so irresistible."

"I'm going to give you the best pedicure you've ever had."

We both laugh at the lie. It's no secret I'm no good at doing girlie stuff.

CHAPTER thirty three

Cin

I need to be fair to Trevor and go through with my plan, I tell myself for the millionth time. I've put it off for the last three weeks. No more waiting. I parked down the street from Trevor's house nearly an hour and a half ago, but I can't bring myself to do what I came here for. I contemplate a little more before starting the ignition and driving the short distance. I count to twenty, then pick up my cell phone to call Trevor. It's better if I do this now, so he can have time to apply to other colleges.

"Hey, babe," he says.

"Hi."

"What's up?"

"We have to talk."

"I kind of figured that's why you called." He chuckles.

"I'm outside."

"Why didn't you knock on the door, silly?"

"I'd rather we talk in my car."

"Let me guess, you got some new ink and you want to give me a private show?" he jokes.

Trevor was surprised by my impromptu decision to get a tattoo, but he thinks it's the sexiest thing ever—if he only knew the real reason behind it.

"I don't want your family to overhear our conversation."

"What's going on?" His tone turns serious.

"Please come out."

"Give me a few minutes."

"Okay."

A torrent of tears erupts from my eyes the moment he closes the car door.

"Babe, it's okay. We'll get through whatever you're upset about together."

I cry harder.

"Talk to me."

"It's over between us," I wail.

"Did I do something wrong?"

"No, it's me."

"Tell me what I need to do to fix us."

"There's nothing you can do. I need space," I lie.

"Is that the only explanation you're going to give me?" He punches the dashboard. "That's not good enough!"

"I'm doing this for you."

"No, Cin. You're doing this for you!"

"I don't want to hurt you."

"You have a funny way of showing it," he says sarcastically.

"I want the best for you."

"You're what's best for me." He grips the back of my neck and brings me forward to slam his lips to mine.

I turn my head, ending the kiss. "Stop."

"We belong together."

"It's over!" I stare straight ahead, unable to bear the devastation on his face. "We were stupid to think we'd get married one day. There's so much we haven't seen or done. I don't want to wake up one day and be dissatisfied with the choices I've made in my life."

"I chose to attend Lexington University to be with you."

"I didn't ask you to do that."

"I love you so much, Cin."

"I'm sorry." I have to remain steadfast. Trevor is my first love, so he'll always have a place in my heart.

"Who is he?"

"There's no one."

"You're lying."

"There isn't," I insist.

The school will become a war zone if Trevor finds out Art is the reason we broke up. I need to make sure the tenuous peace between the boys is kept, at least until after graduation.

"Do I look like a fucking idiot to you?"

"It's the truth!"

"It better be because if I find out otherwise, he's fucking dead." He leaves the car, slamming the door shut.

ART

Over the last several weeks, Cin has become more and more distant, spending the night with friends when she should be in my bed. I thought we'd be fucking like rabbits since she and Trevor are no longer an item. Friday night was the last time I had the pleasure of coming inside her, which was a week ago yesterday. She's never stayed away this long. Having her only once a week isn't nearly enough for me. When I see Trevor in school or around the house, I want to tell him how good his ex-girlfriend's pussy is. The only thing stopping me is Cin. She might stop talking to me altogether. And if Ricky and her mother find out about us, they'll send me packing for sure. Whenever I ask what her problem is, she makes up some bullshit excuse.

If Cin thinks she's about to end it with me, she has another thing coming. It's about time I nip this in the fucking bud. She doesn't know who the hell she's dealing with. I'm done lying to myself. I want all of her. She loves me, though there's a possibility she made the declaration in the heat of the moment. No, I can't believe that. I want to become a better person for her, and I'm willing to do whatever it takes. I'm finally sleeping through the night, and I stopped cutting because of her. I can't be without her. If she rejects me, I'm going to fucking lose it.

Cin got home thirty minutes ago, but I wait for Ricky and Missy to leave for their morning deliveries before I silently creep up the stairs.

I twist the doorknob but find it locked. "Open this damn door, or I'll bulldoze right the fuck through it."

"I'm busy," she whispers.

"You have three fucking seconds to open this motherfucking door."

She cracks it open. "I'm about to head out."

I nudge the door, but she holds firm. *Aww, that's cute.* She thinks she can keep me out. I shoulder my way in, sending her stumbling back. She's only wearing a bra and panties. My God, I want to fuck her until she becomes bedridden.

"I want to know what your fucking problem is, and don't tell me everything is fine."

"I'm busy. I have a track meet this morning."
"You're staying away because of me."
"I don't have time for this. I'm going to be late."
"Make time. I'm not letting you leave until we talk about us."
"There is no us."
A knife to the heart would've hurt less.
"You said you loved me."
"I do."
"I thought you broke up with Trevor to be with me."
"No, I didn't."
She turns the invisible knife counterclockwise, inflicting the most damage.
"You still love him?"
When she doesn't answer, I grab her ponytail and jerk her head back. I don't care if I hurt her. She needs to feel the same pain she's causing me.
"My pain is your pain."
"It has to be this way," she sobs. "We're going different places in life."
"I'll follow wherever you go."
"You have to find yourself first."
"What the fuck is that supposed to mean?"
"You're just starting to overcome your demons."
"I need you."
"You're not ready for a serious relationship."

"Do you think I'm going to stand by and let you live happily ever after? Fuck that. You aren't Cinderella, and I'm no Prince Charming." I slide my hand into her panties and grab her feminine softness.

Moans escape her parted lips as I kiss along her exposed neck.

"No! Fucking no! You broke up with Trevor for him?"

A pissed-off Josh stands in the doorway. I turn to face him, sure to block Cin's scantily dressed figure from his sight.

"Josh." Cin moves around me.

I shove her towards the closet. "Put some fucking clothes on."

"How could you do this to Trevor? He points at me. "And with *him* of all people?"

"I'm not good for Trevor. That's why I had to break up with him."

"I said put on some fucking clothes!"

She hurriedly moves to obey.

"Trevor will be heartbroken," Josh says.

"I know," she replies.

"Don't look at her. Look at me," I say.

"I'll dislocate your fucking jaw."

"If you're ready to get paralyzed, bring it."

We move towards each other, but Cin positions herself between us, preventing contact. She still doesn't have on bottoms, but at least she put on a shirt.

"Your righteous anger on your friend's behalf is fake as shit," I say.

"You wouldn't know how to be someone's friend."

"Do you kiss all your friends' girlfriends?"

He turns white as a sheet. "You told him," he accuses.

"I didn't."

"Someone's cranky because they never had the pleasure of sampling Cin's sweet pussy."

"Josh, go back to your room. What Art and I had is over."

"No, it's not," I say at the same time Josh says, "That's not what it looks like."

"Josh, go."

"I will when he does."

"I'm not going anywhere, but you are."

"Like hell."

"I wonder how Trevor will react if he finds out his best friend has a thing for his ex-girl."

Josh and I engage in a short staring contest before he averts his eyes and walks out.

"Get on the bed and spread your legs."

"Art…"

I toss her on the bed. "Enough talking."

"I have a track meet."

"It's been a week. I can't wait a second longer. I'll be quick, I promise." I flip her over. "Head down, ass up."

I never thought I'd be so happy to enter the gates of hell. Her scorching hot pussy has me under a spell—damn witch. I fuck us both into a stupor. One way or another, Cin will be mine.

Chapter thirty five

Cin

Not only was I almost an hour late to the track meet, I didn't bring my A game. Art's version of a quickie was nearly a half hour. I let my coach and team down, completely bombing. Anneli was very vocal about her disappointment, using every profanity in the dictionary—some I've never heard. I've been staying with her all week, only going home this morning to get more clothes. I walk into Anneli's bedroom, prepared to have my head bitten off. She lies across her bed, watching television.

"Why were you late?" She doesn't take her eyes from the screen.

"I told you—"

"You're fashion retarded. You grab any article of clothing you get your hands on first. It takes you less than sixty seconds to pack a bag, so don't tell me that's the reason again."

I remove the chair stationed at her small work table and bring it beside her bed before dropping into it.

"I told myself it's only fair to let them both go."

"But you can't let Art go."

"No."

"You love him."

"He has my heart."

"Talk about complicated."

"I was late because of him. It was only a matter of time before he confronted me."

"What happened?"

"I tried to be strong, but with him, my defenses disappear. He called me out on my bullshit, and we argued. That's not even the half of it."

Anneli scoots to the edge of her bed. "I'm all ears."

"Josh caught us kissing."

"Do you think he'll tell Trevor?"

"No, not with the threat Art left hanging over his head," I say.

"What threat?"

"Remember I told you about Lilah and her big mouth."

"Oh yeah, I forgot about that."

"Art threatened to tell Trevor."
"Your life is becoming a reality TV show."
"Tell me about it."
"Can I be honest with you?"
"Always."
"What you're doing to Trevor is really shitty."
"I know. I'm a horrible person."

The gossip mill couldn't wait to spread rumors about our breakup, making going to school awkward for the last few weeks. The classes Trevor and I share are thick with tension. He doesn't speak to me at all. If our eyes happen to connect, he quickly looks away. Most days, I steer clear of the cafeteria, preferring to eat lunch away from prying eyes. Plus, I don't want to make everyone at the table uncomfortable. I've seen Trevor around the house, hanging out with Josh on the occasion I'm home to spend time with my mom or pack more clothes.

"Love is the deadliest poison known to humankind. It makes people do crazy shit, and once the emotion sinks its claws in, it travels through the bloodstream, refusing to offer freedom. There's good and bad love, Cin. Art can only offer you the latter. I'm not telling you this to scare you, but as a friend."

"I see a future with him."
"What?"

"You asked me before if I saw a future with Trevor or Art, but I didn't have an answer then because I was so confused."

"Are you sure?"

"I know it won't be easy, but he's worth it."

"If you and Art go public, shit is going to hit the fan."

"By the time Trevor finds out, it won't matter anymore."

"Will Art keep his mouth shut?"

"Yeah. I'll talk to him tomorrow."

"For everyone's sake, I hope you're right."

"Me too." I clutch my head as a wave of dizziness overcomes me.

"What's the matter?"

"I feel sick again."

Anneli circles her arm around my shoulder. "You've been sick off and on since Tuesday."

"I'm going to throw up." I race to the bathroom with Anneli on my heels.

She holds my hair back while I retch into the toilet. When I'm done, I sit on my bottom, barely able to hold my head up. Anneli wets a washcloth, wiping my sweaty face.

"Thank you."

"Jesus. Your breath smells rancid." Anneli pinches her nostrils closed.

"Kiss my ass."

"You should go to the doctor."

"No, it's just a virus. It'll pass."

"I don't think you have a virus. You're fine one moment, then the next, you're sick as a dog."

"If it doesn't pass by next week, I'll schedule an appointment."

"I'll help you brush your teeth, then off to bed you go."

"You're the best."

"I know."

I feel horrible. Some sleep will do me good.

When I wake, the hour is late and Anneli is fast asleep next to me. My growling stomach forces me to venture to the kitchen for a snack of saltine crackers and water since I'm still a little lightheaded and surprisingly tired, even after several hours of rest. I walk to the sofa and lie down, too weak to attempt walking upstairs. There, I fall back asleep.

"Cin."

I blink my eyes open to Anneli hovering over my prone form.

"Morning," I say.

"What are you doing sleeping on the sofa?"

"I came down for a snack but was too tired to go back to your bedroom."

"I didn't wake you for dinner because my mom said to let you sleep after I told her how sick you were."

"That's okay. I probably wouldn't have been able to eat a heavy meal, anyway."

"How are you feeling this morning?"

I slowly move to a sitting position afraid of another dizzy spell. "The dizziness and queasiness are gone."

"Good."

"Why are you dressed?"

"I'm going to the mall."

"This early?"

"It's nearly noon, sleepyhead."

"Oh."

"Are you up to going?"

"Yeah, I feel a lot better."

"Get dressed. I'll wait for you down here."

"I'll be ready in twenty."

"Honestly, Anneli, was buying eight pairs of booty shorts really necessary?" I ask as we leave the clothing store.

I'm becoming more fatigued by the second.

"Umm, yeah. You've seen my ass. It's made for them."

I roll my eyes. "Summer isn't for another two and a half months."

"It'll be here before you know it. You should've bought some for yourself."

"Trust me. No one wants to see my boney ass in booty shorts."

"True, you have a flat one."

"Oh, fuck you." I hit her arm.

"Hey, I'm only agreeing with you."

"Gee, thanks."

"I want to check out a few more stores, then we can eat dinner at the food court."

"The thought of eating anything makes me sick. I need to rest."

We sit on a nearby bench.

"Are you ready to leave?"

"I don't want to ruin your shopping spree."

"I can finish shopping anytime. My best friend comes first."

"It is better if I don't puke in front of all these people."

"I'm going to ask you something, but I don't want you to freak out."

"Well, it's too late because that comment has me freaking out."

"I'll ask you when we get back to my house."

"No, ask me now."

"Okay. Here it goes. When was your last period?"

"Like a week ago, but it wasn't a normal period, only two days of spotting. It's because of the stress with everything going on."

"When was your last normal period?"

"I think a week before Valentine's Day. Why?"

"Your symptoms are consistent with pregnancy."

"Being sick doesn't mean I'm pregnant."

"That's true, but you should buy a couple pregnancy tests to rule out the possibility."

"I'm beyond freaked out now."

"Have you been taking your birth control pills?"

"Yes. I mean no, not on time. Sometimes I forget, so I double or triple up. My doctor said it's okay to do that."

"Doing that probably decreases effectiveness."

"If I'm pregnant, the father could be either Trevor or Art."

"Let's take this one step at a time."

"Okay."

God, I hope I'm not pregnant.

Chapter thirty six

Cin

I drive home in disbelief. On our way out of the mall, I ran to the nearest garbage can and puked my guts out—a very embarrassing moment I never want to relive. By the time the third pregnancy test showed a positive result, I was hysterical. I'm going to have a baby, and it's a big fucking deal. How can I start college in the fall? I'll have to tell Trevor about Art. I can't let him think this baby is his when there's a fifty percent chance it isn't. I made a complete mess of my life. Anneli tried to calm me down and persuade me to stay the night to consider my options before making a hasty decision, but it's already been made. I couldn't live with myself if I got an abortion, and adoption is out of the question. I would always wonder about the baby I gave away.

Anneli didn't want me driving in this state, but I needed to get home and talk to my mom. She'll be so disappointed in me, but no matter what, I know she'll stick by my side.

I notice Trevor's truck alongside Josh's as I park my car. Shit. Having to see Trevor after learning of my impending motherhood less than a half hour ago is unnerving. Art's motorcycle is nowhere in sight, so at least I have a reprieve from him for the time being. I enter the house, heading to the kitchen to get a drink before having this very difficult conversation with my mom. The bathroom door opens, bringing me face-to-face with Art. He takes hold of my wrist and drags me into the bathroom. He pushes me forward, pressing my thighs into the sink. My eyes connect with his in the mirror.

"Where's your motorcycle?"

"In the backyard."

"Why?"

"I wanted to catch you off guard. You should've come home last night." He licks my neck, then delivers a stinging bite. "I warned you yesterday. No more staying away."

His magical fingers slide into my bottoms to circle my clit, while his lips create a tingling path from my shoulder to my ear. I moan, dropping my head back onto his chest. The sight of him working his hand between my legs in the mirror is so fucking erotic.

"Do you want me to fuck you?" he asks in a guttural voice.

I bite my bottom lip, nodding.

"I need to hear you say it."

"I want you to fuck me."

"How bad do you want me to fuck you?"

"I want you so bad, I'm willing to risk losing everything to have you."

I whimper as he increases the pressure on my sensitive clit.

He steps back just enough to pull down my bottoms and panties. I bite my fist to prevent myself from screaming as his thick erection penetrates my body until he can go no farther. He wraps his strong hand around my throat.

"I'm going to savor your pussy this time."

He's the storm and I'm the rain. Without one, the other can't exist. Art slowly withdraws from my body, then thrusts forward at the same speed. It's the sweetest torture. My eyes are glued to his beautiful green eyes.

"Do you love me?" he asks.

"Now and forever."

I clutch the sink as his strokes become faster and more ferocious.

"How can you make me lose control like this?"

My climax consumes me, expanding from my core and reducing me to a state of sensuality I've never felt before.

"I want to spend the rest of my life with you," he groans, filling me with his cum.

He steps back and sits on the edge of the bathtub, watching me clean myself with tissue.

"Aren't you going to clean up a bit?" I ask.

"Nah, I like having the smell of you on me."

His piercing gaze makes me feel self-conscious. "A little privacy?"

"Not a chance."

"Fine." I turn sideways to block his view.

"No, you don't." He grasps my hips, guiding me to face him. "I'm enjoying the show."

"Asshole." I laugh, throwing the tissue in the toilet. "I'm done."

"After graduation, it's me and you. I'm coming with you to California."

If only California were still a possibility for me.

"Say something," he demands.

I'm not ready to tell him I'm pregnant yet.

"Look at me." He grasps my chin, lifting my head to meet his eyes. "You don't want me to go?"

"I have to tell you something."

"Okay, tell me."

"I will, just not now."

"Why the fuck not?"

"Give me some time, okay? I promise I'll tell you soon."

"I'll give you one week, Cin, and then I expect answers."

"Okay, one week."

ART

I can't keep still, so I do sets of pushups. She looked guilty. Maybe she wants to get back with Trevor. Well, too fucking bad. That'll only happen over my cold dead body. There's no going back. I refuse to share her again. She's mine. I had no idea being shipped to North Carolina would change my outlook on life, and I have Cin to thank for that. She already has my heart, but I'd give that girl much more.

"Hey," Ricky greets me.

"Just because I left the door open a little doesn't mean you have an invitation to come inside."

"I need to speak to you in my office."

Oh fuck, this can't be good. I follow him into his office, surprised to find the old man there. Ricky closes the door, then perches on the corner of his desk.

"What the fuck is going on here?"

"It's better if you have a seat." Ricky motions towards an empty chair.

I remain where I am.

"Suit yourself," Ricky says.

"Arthur, are you using cocaine again?" the old man asks.

The motherfucker has never been good at subtlety.

"I thought we were going to ease into the conversation." Ricky sighs.

"No, I'm not," I reply.

"Show him."

Ricky pulls a small clear baggie from his pocket. "This was under the dining room table. Is it yours?"

"Yes." There's no point in lying. Damn, I never thought about looking for the baggie.

"So, you're on drugs again!" The old man springs to his feet.

"Sit back down, before you have a heart attack and find yourself alongside your son in a nursing home."

"How can you be so calm about this?" Ricky asks.

"I was going to get high, but I didn't."

"And we're supposed to believe you?" my grandfather asks.

"I don't give a damn what you believe, but to get you off my back, I'll take a drug test." I walk towards the door, considering the matter over.

"You brought drugs into my house with the purpose of getting high, regardless if you didn't," Ricky says. "That's a big fucking deal."

"Give me a fucking break. It happened on Cole's birthday."

"Shit, I'm sorry, Art. I forgot about his birthday."

"I'm sure you're not the only one." My gaze settles on my red-faced grandfather. "Now if there's nothing else…"

"There is," Ricky says.

"Oh goody."

He pulls my razor from his pocket. "We know you've been cutting yourself."

"How can you mutilate yourself like some deranged lunatic?" the old man shouts.

The cuts have healed. Still, there would be no mistaking how the scars happened.

"Who told you?"

"It doesn't matter," Ricky answers.

The only person who knew about my cutting and what happened on Cole's birthday is Cin. Would she have told the secrets she promised to keep? The changes in her behavior are beginning to add up. She didn't seem thrilled about me going to California. I rush from the room.

"Cin!" I shout, storming up the stairs.

She stabbed me in the fucking back. I want her to look into my eyes and admit her betrayal.

Ricky and the old man race behind me. Josh and Trevor step into the hall as I reach the top of the stairs.

"What the hell are you doing?" Ricky grasps my arm.

I jerk from his hold and glance to the left when I see a door opening. There she is, the girl who ripped my heart in half, standing beside her mother. Cin's face and eyes are puffy. It's clear she's been crying.

"You fucking betrayed me!"

"I didn't." Cin cautiously walks towards me.

"Stay away from him," Missy says.

"Mom, it's okay."

"Don't fucking lie to me!" I yell in her face.

"Get the fuck away from her," Trevor growls.

"Are you going to make me?"

"Yeah."

I wave him over. "It's about time I fucked you up, anyway."

"Josh, take Trevor to your room," Ricky says.

"Do you want to know why Cin left you?" I ask.

"Please don't do this," Cin begs.

"I've been swimming in her pussy almost every night like it's a fucking ocean for months, even when she bled between her damn legs. You wouldn't know anything about that, would you? Bloody pussy is for big boys." My dark soul sings in triumph at the stricken look on his face.

"Tell me he's lying," Trevor says.

"I'm so sorry."

"How could you?" he shouts.

"Arthur, it's time for us to leave," my grandfather says.

"But I'm having the time of my life."

"Dad, you should never have brought him here."

"She has the most delicious pussy I ever had the pleasure of sticking my dick into… raw."

An anguished scream leaves Trevor's throat before he attacks me. I crash into the wall, leaving a dent. He punches me in the face, knocking a tooth loose. My mouth fills with blood. I get in a few good hits before we're pried apart.

The old man and Josh restrain me in front of the stairs, while Ricky struggles to keep Trevor contained at the end of the hall.

"I'm going to kill you!"

"Did Josh tell you he kissed her? He's been holding a torch for her a long time."

Trevor looks from Josh to Cin, seeing the truth of my words in their expressions. He breaks free of Ricky, charging us. My grandfather jumps out of the way. Josh falls over the banister, an agonizing sound leaving his mouth when he hits the floor below. Trevor and I tumble down the stairs, continuing our fight in the living room until we're torn away from each other a second time. The old man has Trevor in a headlock by the door while

Ricky holds me in a bear hug from behind, next to a screeching Josh.

"My leg is broken," he bellows.

Cin kneels beside him. "Mom, call for an ambulance."

"We fucked in there." I nod my head towards the bathroom door. "Not even an hour ago." I can't resist pissing Trevor off further.

"Shut the fuck up," Cin hisses.

Missy stands beside Ricky and me as she speaks to the dispatcher. Trevor manages to bend over, picking up one of Ricky's work boots before launching it across the living room. Missy is struck in the face, causing her to crash into the wall, knocking her unconscious.

"What have you done?" Cin cries, crawling over to her mother.

"It was an accident," Trevor says in a distraught voice.

"Trevor, for God's sake, go home!" Ricky yells.

He leaves, defeated and with a broken heart. Ricky releases his hold on me to attend to Josh and Missy.

I kneel in front of Cin. "You gave me a little piece of heaven, but now you want to take it away. If I'm going back to hell, I'm taking you with me."

She glares at me with hate flashing in her eyes. "You should've died the day you slit your wrists."

Her words have the same impact as a bullet to the head. I will never show weakness to another person again. Like Trevor, I leave without saying another word, defeated, but not with a broken heart. The useless organ is now filled with rage.

thank you for reading

That was one hell of a ride. I hope you enjoyed it as much as I did. Writing this book was not easy—it took me down unknown paths, causing me to continuously second guess myself. Eventually, I found the perfect balance. If you thought this book was an emotional roller coaster, you haven't seen anything yet, so stay tuned for the conclusion of Art and Cin's story. Don't forget to leave a review and read my other books! Connect with me on social media:

Facebook – Author Lorrain Allen

Instagram – author_lorrain_allen

TikTok – authorlorrainallen

Twitter – AuthorLAllen

about the author

Lorrain Allen currently resides on the East Coast. She has one amazing, albeit spoiled, son. She loves to get away from the world by losing herself in a book. Her long-term goal is to pen dark, erotic, paranormal, contemporary, new adult, and young adult romances. The subject matters of her books are controversial, but what's life without a little controversy?

other books

Standalones

Slippery When Wet: When Adults Play

The Games We Play

Consumed: A Dark Stalker Age Gap Romance

Maverick's Madness: A Dark High School Bully Romance

Living in Cin Duet

When Art Rises: Living in Cin (A Dark High School Romance)

When Art Falls: Living in Cin (A Dark Romance)

A Little Taste of Sin Series

Sweet Peach

Midas Touch

Gods of Ruin MC Series

Beautiful Hate: A Dark MC Romance

www.authorlorrainallen.com